M000199054

Forever

Takes a While

Colt and Cassie
Summer Lake Seasons Book Five

By SJ McCoy

A Sweet n Steamy Romance

Published by Xenion, Inc

Copyright © 2020 SJ McCoy

FOREVER TAKES A WHILE Copyright © SJ McCoy 2020

All rights reserved. Except as permitted under the U.S. Copyright Act of 1976, no part of this publication may be reproduced, distributed, or transmitted in any form, or by any means, or stored in a database or retrieval system without prior written consent of the author.

Published by Xenion, Inc.
First paperback edition 2020
www.sjmccoy.com

This book is a work of fiction. Names, characters, places, and events are figments of the author's imagination, fictitious, or are used fictitiously. Any resemblance to actual events, locales or persons living or dead is coincidental.

Cover Design by Dana Lamothe of Designs by Dana
Editor: Mitzi Pummer Carroll
Proofreaders: Aileen Blomberg, Marisa Nichols, Traci Atkinson.

ISBN: 978-1-946220-65-3

Dedication

For Sam. Sometimes, life really is too short. Few.

xxx

Chapter One

Colt pushed open the door to the bakery and stopped dead in his tracks when he saw her.

Cassie.

She'd made a big point of avoiding him for months. They hadn't exchanged more than a couple of words since she'd come back to the lake. That spoke volumes. It took a determined effort to avoid anyone in such a small town as Summer Lake, and, considering the fact that they shared the same group of friends, he knew the effort Cassie was going to was monumental.

In the beginning, he'd tried to talk to her; he'd made several attempts to pull her aside. She didn't want to straighten things out between them? He didn't like that, but he could respect it. But refusing to even speak to him was starting to chafe him. He'd always thought of Cassie as a mature person—even when they were kids—but, in his mind, her behavior since she'd come back to town was nothing less than childish.

He sucked in a deep breath and forced himself to avoid looking at her, instead smiling at Renée and April, who were standing behind the counter looking uncomfortable.

"Good morning, ladies." In his mind, the greeting included Cassie. It was up to her if she chose to ignore it.

Renée smiled warmly. "Morning, Colt. I have your order ready."

Cassie picked up a box from the counter and turned to leave. Colt pressed his lips together to stop himself from making one more attempt to get through to her.

To his surprise, she gave him a brief nod as she passed him on the way out. That was something, at least.

When the door closed behind her, he let out the breath he didn't realize he'd been holding.

"I wish the two of you would just get over it," said Renée. "It makes it difficult for everyone. You were such good friends. I don't know what happened, but I wish you'd let it go."

Colt scowled at her. "You're talking to the wrong guy. I let it go years ago. Cassie's the one who won't talk to me."

"Yeah, sorry. I know that." Renée gave him a sad smile. "But you've always been the peacemaker. The guy who can smooth over disagreements and bring everyone back together when there's any trouble. Why can't you do it now?"

"I wish I knew. If I could make her talk to me, I'd love to make things right, but that nod she gave me when she left? That's the most she's said to me in years." Colt shook his head sadly. "I think I have to resign myself to the fact that she's not interested."

"Interested?" Renée raised an eyebrow. "Would you still be?"

"Not like that. I meant she's not even interested in talking to me, in being friends again. Anyway, you said you've got everything ready? I need to get those donuts to the guys."

Renée handed him a box that contained two dozen sugary reasons to hurry his ass to work. "Thanks."

"Are you coming out with everyone this weekend?" asked April.

"You mean to the Boathouse on Saturday night?"

"Yes. Clay's going to sing with Eddie and Chase. He hasn't done it for a while, and I think he likes it when it's quieter."

"In that case, yeah. I'll definitely be there."

"Great. We'll see you then."

He slid the box of donuts onto the passenger seat and headed to work. He slowed just before he reached the end of Main Street when he saw Cassie walking. Why the hell was she on foot in this weather?

He knew that she'd more than likely blow him off, but he had to stop and ask if she wanted a ride.

He let down the passenger window when he reached her.

"Cassie."

She glanced at him but kept on walking.

He pursed his lips and crawled along beside her. "Come on. It's freezing out there. Let me give you a ride?"

She turned and met his gaze. It wasn't the hostile look he'd grown used to seeing from her. Instead, he could see hesitation in her eyes.

"Go on." He smiled. "You don't have to say a word to me if you don't want to. But I know how much you hate the cold. And if you keep walking, you're going to freeze your ass off by the time you get to work."

His heart started to race when she stopped. He brought the car to a stop beside her and waited.

"Thank you." She opened the door and slid into the passenger seat.

"You're welcome." He pulled away, wishing that the medical center was at least five miles away. He needed time to get her to talk. "How've you been?"

She turned and looked at him but didn't reply.

"Jesus, Cassie. Say something. Anything. But please talk to me. This is driving me nuts!"

She blew out a sigh. "There's nothing left to say between us."

"Why?!" He gripped the steering wheel and tried to reel in his frustration.

She stared out the windshield and didn't even look as though she planned to answer.

"Why are you so angry at me?"

She shrugged. "I'm not."

"So why won't you talk to me?"

"Because there's no point."

He blew out a frustrated sigh. "What's the point in not talking to me? Why can't we be friends?"

He glanced over at her and was stunned to see that her eyes were brimming with tears.

"Cassie?"

"Dammit, Colt! Why couldn't you just let it be? This!" She swiped at her eyes angrily. "This is the reason I don't want to talk to you. It's the reason we can't be friends."

He didn't understand. "Because I make you cry?"

She nodded. "Yeah. Because I don't trust myself to be around you. I'm sorry, okay? I'm sorry for everything that happened. And I'm sorry that I've been so damned childish since I came back here. All I was trying to do was avoid this— avoid letting you see that I'm still such a mess."

"Cassie." He reached across and touched her arm, but she pulled it away as if he'd scalded her. "Why?" He didn't understand. He got that she was still mad at him, but he didn't get why it would upset her so much.

She let out a strangled little laugh. "Because, apparently, I'm an idiot."

They'd reached the medical center, but Colt didn't want to let her out of the car now. He drove by the entrance, planning to go around the block.

"We're there."

He shook his head. "I'm guessing you start at eight. You're early. You wouldn't have arrived for at least ten minutes if you were walking."

She shrugged. "So, what? You're planning to drive me around for ten minutes?"

"Yep." He glanced over at her and caught the hint of a smile.

"You're still stubborn, then?"

That made him smile back at her. "Not as stubborn as you are."

"I'm not stubborn; I'm just determined. I have to be if I'm going to get where I want to go in life."

All the hairs on Colt's arms stood up. How many times had she said that to him when they were kids? It was her go-to. It was true, as well. She'd been determined that she was going to be a doctor, and here she was. "Is this where you want to be?"

Her mouth opened and closed, and fresh tears filled her eyes. It made him grip the steering wheel tighter. He'd only meant did she want to be a doctor back here in Summer Lake, but now he wondered if she thought he was asking if she wanted to be here—with him.

"Cassie, would you please tell me what your problem is?"

She sighed, making him hope that she was finally going to tell him. "My problem is that you won't respect my desire to have nothing to do with you anymore. The only thing we have left to say to each other is goodbye."

That felt like a dagger through his heart. He'd hoped that they were about to make a breakthrough—to find a way back to being friends. He'd almost come to terms with knowing that she'd never even consider being with him again, but he couldn't imagine her living here at the lake and not even being part of his life in some small way.

He turned the last corner that brought them back to the medical center. "Is that really what you want?" Even to him, his voice sounded sharp and angry. It wasn't anger—it was pain—but it was better that she didn't know that.

She nodded. "It's for the best."

"Okay, then." He brought the car to a stop. "I don't understand, but it seems that doesn't matter to you. I thought … well, I thought a lot of things, but I guess none of those matter now either. I've always respected what you want. You know that." He turned to look at her. She was even more beautiful now that she was older. In his mind, she'd always been the most beautiful girl in the world. But he'd loved her for so much more than her looks. "There's so much I want to say, but if the only thing you want to hear from me is goodbye. Then …" He couldn't help it. He reached across and touched her cheek. "Goodbye, Cassie."

She let out a strangled sound and scrambled out of the car, slamming the door closed behind her and hurrying away.

He sat there and watched until she disappeared through the door, feeling as though his heart was breaking all over again. Damn. He'd told himself that he was over her. He had to be. It'd been so long. But even through the last few months when she'd refused to talk to him, his heart had refused to accept that they didn't have another chapter to write.

He blew out a sigh and gripped the steering wheel with shaky hands. Now, it seemed, he didn't have any choice but to accept it.

Cassie stumbled blindly into the waiting room. She was doing her best not to let herself cry. If she could just make it to her office ...

"Cassie! What's wrong?" Abbie, the receptionist, came hurrying out from behind the desk. "What is it?"

She sniffed and tried to compose herself. "Nothing. I'm ... it's ..." So much for not letting herself cry! Tears were streaming down her cheeks.

"Come and sit down." Abbie took her arm and led her into her office. "Did something happen? Are you okay?"

Cassie sucked in a deep breath and forced herself to get a grip. She handed the box of pastries to Abbie and gave her a weak smile. "I'm sorry. Everything's fine. I'm just being an idiot. Do you want to take those through to the back, and I'll come and join you in a minute?"

Abbie frowned. "No. I don't. I want you to tell me what the hell is going on. I'm worried."

"There's no need. Like I said. I'm just being an idiot."

"What about?"

"Nothing."

Abbie put her hands on her hips. "Come on, Cassie. I've done my best to keep my nose out and respect your privacy. But you can't get into a state like this and expect me not to care." Her expression softened. "I do care, you know. I just want you to be okay, and you're obviously not."

Cassie's eyes filled with tears again, and she swiped at them angrily. "I will be. I promise. I think you know the reason that I've been so difficult since I came back to town."

Abbie nodded. "Colt?"

"Yep."

"Can't you just talk to him? I know you say you'd rather avoid him, but surely it'd be better to talk and sort out whatever you need to."

"That's exactly what I just did."

"Oh! And it didn't make things better?"

Cassie laughed. "It did. I know it doesn't look like it, but it did. It just makes me sad, that's all."

"Do you want to explain?"

"Not really, no, but I will. I've been avoiding him—"

"Err, yeah. I know that much. So does everyone else in town."

"I know, and I'm sorry. I know I've been acting like an idiot. But … I couldn't do it. I couldn't talk to him because I knew that I'd end up like this."

"Like this?"

"Bawling my eyes out and a total mess. I'm supposed to be cool, calm, collected Cassie, the one who has it all together and can cope with anything. But I'm not. Not when it comes to Colt. The only thing I can't cope with is being around him and not being with him anymore. He was my best friend, my everything. I don't know how to be just his friend; I don't want to be just his friend. That's all there could ever be between us now, and I'd rather have nothing."

"And this morning, you told him that?"

"I did. And it was the saddest thing I've ever done. He didn't understand, and I don't think it even bothered him that much."

Abbie looked skeptical.

"He said if the only thing I wanted to hear him say was goodbye …" Her voice wavered. "Then he'd say it."

Abbie came and put her arm around her shoulders as a fresh wave of tears rolled down her cheeks.

"You lied, didn't you?"

Cassie met her gaze.

"You didn't want him to say goodbye. You wanted him to say that he loves you."

Cassie closed her eyes, but the tears leaked out between her lashes as she nodded. "I don't want to be around him because I know he doesn't feel that way anymore. It hurts too much, Abbie."

Abbie wrapped her in a hug, and for a moment, Cassie leaned against her and closed her eyes. It wasn't her way to lean on anyone, in any sense, but at that moment, it helped to know that she had a friend.

"I screwed it all up a long time ago. I wish I could go back and do things differently."

"You can't go back, but maybe you could do things differently now?"

She shook her head. "It's too late."

~ ~ ~

Colt felt as though the day passed in a blur. By the time he got home, he couldn't remember anything he'd done, not since Cassie had gotten out of the car this morning.

He blew out a sigh and went to get himself a beer from the fridge. Why did she have to close the door on them completely? Better question: why had he made her get into the car? Made her talk to him? It'd been bad enough before, knowing that she was avoiding him. But that had still left him with hope—hope that, at some point, she'd soften toward him and they'd be able to talk their way past it like they always used to do. But no. He'd gone and pushed it, pushed too far so that the only choice she'd had was to tell him the truth. She didn't want him in her life—in any capacity.

He took a drink of his beer and wandered into the living room. He looked at the picture above the fireplace. He knew she'd love it. Santorini. They'd planned to go there someday. He'd gone alone a few years ago and spent the whole time wishing she was with him.

He set his beer down and headed for the shower. He needed to get out of the house. If he spent the evening here, he'd only end up wallowing in memories.

It was only seven o'clock when he got to the Boathouse. It was quiet, but that was no surprise on a Monday. The girl behind the bar greeted him with a smile.

"Well, hello, Deputy. Have you come to keep me company on a slow night?"

He forced a smile. He had kept her company on a couple of nights—and they'd been anything but slow. He'd told her that things weren't going to go anywhere between them, but she wasn't shy about letting him know that she was interested in whatever he did want to offer.

"I've come for dinner." That meant he could go and sit in a booth and not have to stay at the bar and talk to her.

She shrugged. "Okay. Seat yourself."

He made his way to one of the booths in the back. It wasn't likely that too many folks would be out tonight, but he'd rather be out of sight if anyone he knew came in.

He shook his head in disbelief when he saw Ivan come out of the bathroom. He could hardly hide from him.

"Colt. What are you doing here?"

"Getting some dinner. I didn't feel like cooking tonight."

Ivan grinned. "Awesome. Mind if I join you? Abbie's mom's in town, and I brought myself out of the way so they can have a girly evening."

"Sure."

Ivan followed him to a booth. "You can tell me to buzz off if you want. You don't seem thrilled."

"Sorry. It's not you. It's me."

Ivan laughed. "You sound like you're breaking up with me."

Colt shrugged.

"What is it?" Ivan's smile faded. "What's wrong, bud?"

Colt shrugged again. Ivan had become a good friend, but he didn't feel like spilling his guts to him.

"With anyone else, I'd say the look on your face meant girl trouble. But I know that's not the case with you … is it? It is, isn't it?"

Colt rolled his eyes. "Jesus. Can you leave it alone?"

"Whoa!" Ivan held his hands up. "Sorry! I didn't mean to be an asshole about it. I just … I'm surprised."

"I'm the one who's being an asshole. Sorry for biting your head off."

"That's okay. You don't want to talk about it. I can respect that."

His choice of words took Colt straight back. Cassie had told him that he needed to respect her desire to have nothing to do with him. He swallowed around the lump that formed in his throat. He would respect her, but he'd need a while to come to terms with it.

He looked at Ivan. "Thanks. Maybe one day soon I'll ask if I can bend your ear, but for tonight, I'm just looking to distract myself." He smiled. "Or now that you're here, you can distract me. Tell me a story, tell me what's happening in your world. Tell me anything?"

Ivan smiled. "Want to hear about the latest campaign we're running?"

Colt raised an eyebrow, not sure that he did.

"It's all about getting backpacks for foster kids."

Colt frowned, hoping that he wasn't talking about bulletproof backpacks. As a law enforcement officer, he saw enough of the darker side of life, but he knew full well that the darker side of Summer Lake was a shining light compared to many parts of the country. He didn't want to think about any of that tonight.

"Did you know that when foster kids are moved, most of them only ever have garbage bags to put their stuff in?"

It took Colt a minute to register what he was saying.

Ivan nodded. "I know in the grand scheme of things, having a backpack to put your stuff in doesn't seem like much, but think about it. It's a big deal to them."

Colt smiled. He could see that. "I know you're not touting for business, but sign me up. I want to help."

Ivan smiled. "You can stop into the office any time you like and make a donation. How about that?"

"Sure. I'll come in on my day off."

They both looked up when the server came to take their order. Once she'd gone, Ivan raised an eyebrow at him. "Are you sure you want me to tell you about the backpacks?"

"I'm sure. Those kids have much more important problems than I do. I want to hear what you're doing and how I can help."

Chapter Two

Cassie stood out in front of the medical center at the end of the day. She was more than ready to go home. It had been an uneventful day as far as patients went, but she was still reeling from her encounter with Colt this morning.

Normally, she stayed late on a Monday, but she was hoping that her car would be ready. She'd dropped it at the shop before work—if she hadn't, she wouldn't have been walking from the bakery this morning.

She looked up when a car turned in off the street. It was Pete. He'd offered to give her a ride back to the shop; since he and Holly were her closest neighbors, he could also give her a ride home if the car wasn't done yet.

She slid into the passenger seat and greeted him with a smile. "Thanks for this. I really appreciate it."

"No problem. You gave me an excuse to finish early."

Cassie smiled. "Yeah, because you're always looking for one of those."

He laughed. "You know me too well. I admit I've been staying at work too late. It's not fair to Holly. She's home with Noah, and she has work to do, too."

"Well, I'm glad to be the reason that you get home early to her tonight."

"She asked if you want to come over for dinner?"

Cassie adored Holly and little Noah, but having dinner with them was the last thing she wanted to do tonight. "We should do that soon."

Pete raised an eyebrow at her. "I meant tonight. I take it you don't want to?"

"There's no fooling you, is there, Hemming?"

"Nope. I know a brush off when I hear one. And I also know when there's something wrong. Want to tell your Uncle Pete about it?"

She sighed. "Not really. No."

He nodded. "Mind if I guess?"

She didn't answer.

"My guess is that it has something to do with a certain deputy sheriff."

How could he know?

He smiled. "I'm right, aren't I?"

"Yeah, but how?"

"It's not rocket science. The only thing I've ever seen get you down is something to do with Colt. Why don't you just talk to him and sort things out?"

"I did."

Pete frowned. "You obviously didn't sort them out, or you wouldn't be giving off such down and dumpy vibes."

"We did. We agreed that we're just going to stay out of each other's way."

"That's not sorted. That's exactly how things have been. Nothing's changed."

"Everything's changed, Pete. I told him that I don't want anything to do with him."

"Yeah, but you'll get over that in time."

"No. That's what I mean—that there is no getting over it."

"Wow. So, that's it? You're saying never again?"

She nodded.

"Mind if I ask why?"

She shrugged. "You know how things ended between us. I don't want to be his friend. And there can't be anything else."

"Why not?"

"Because he said so."

"Come on, Cass!"

"Come on, what? I chose my career over him."

"Yeah, and now you're both at a different place in life. It doesn't have to be like that anymore—especially now that you're back here."

"I made my choice."

"And you won't change it?"

"I did."

"What do you mean?"

"It doesn't matter." They were almost to the shop. "You can just drop me off. I'm sure they'll be finished by now."

Pete pulled into the parking area and cut the engine. "Nice try, but you don't get rid of me that easily. I'll wait. If it's fixed, I'll follow you home to be sure you get there, and if it's not, I'll give you a ride."

Of course, the car wasn't ready. The guy said that the part he needed should come in on Wednesday, and he should be able to have it finished by Thursday.

Cassie made a face at Pete as she got back into his car. His lips quivered up in a little smirk, but he didn't comment.

They rode in silence until he turned onto West Shore Road.

"Are you seriously going to let a mistake you made years ago stop you from finding happiness now?"

Cassie glanced over at him. "It's not that simple."

"Why not?"

"I realized I'd made a mistake years ago. I told him. Told him I was sorry and that I wanted ... you know."

"And he said no?"

She nodded and swallowed back the tears that were threatening to fall. "Yeah."

Pete shook his head. "I can't believe that. I don't ever remember a time when he wasn't waiting for you."

"He stopped waiting a long time ago."

"You wouldn't say that if you'd been here. If you'd seen him."

Cassie frowned. "Are you trying to make me feel better somehow? I know he gave up on me. And I know about when he was seeing Cara."

Pete laughed. "What, you expected him to remain untouched till you changed your mind?"

"No! I didn't. But you don't know what he said."

"Enlighten me?"

"He said that I'd made my choice, and so he made his. He was happy with her. And that even if he weren't, we'd grown into different people—people who weren't meant to be together."

Pete frowned. "He actually told you that?"

"Yes."

Pete shook his head. "He looked you in the eye and told you he didn't want to get back with you, and he was happy with her?"

"Not exactly."

Pete shot a glance at her. "Here it comes. Tell me what really happened?"

"I called him." Her heart beat a little faster as she remembered that night. Even after years of thinking about it, it'd taken her days to screw up the courage to call him, to tell him that she'd made a huge mistake and ask if there was any way he could forgive her and give her a second chance. "I'd built myself up to it, and then he didn't pick up. So, instead of chickening out completely, I talked to the machine. Told him how wrong I'd been and asked if he could forgive me—if we could try again."

"And he called you back and said no?"

"No. He didn't even want to talk to me himself."

"So, who told you?"

"Cara did."

"Oh, for fuck's sake, Cassie!"

"What?! Can you imagine how much that hurt? After being so close for so many years, he rubbed my nose in it by having his girlfriend call me? And to make matters worse, she was so sweet about it. She was kind when she told me all the things he'd said about him and me being something he'd outgrown and how it'd taken him some time, but he was glad that I'd called things off between us."

"And you know for a fact—without a shadow of a doubt, that he had her call you."

"She called me, didn't she?"

"And you've verified with him that he asked her to?"

"Why would I do that?" Her heart was racing in her chest, knowing that Pete was getting at something—something she should be able to see but couldn't.

"Because maybe he didn't ask her to. Maybe he didn't know the first thing about it. Maybe she picked up your message and decided to take matters into her own hands."

Cassie felt as though she might throw up. "She wouldn't?"

Pete cocked his head to one side. "Wouldn't she? What was it, about two years ago?"

"Two and a half."

"Yeah. I remember they were dating. Cara kept bragging that they were going to get engaged."

Cassie's blood ran cold at that idea.

"Pretty much everyone in town heard that they were going to get engaged—everyone except Colt. At least, not until Dan asked him when the wedding was. Dan likes to play that he's socially inept, but I think he's smarter than the rest of us put together. I think he could see what was going on and wanted Colt to know without having to tell him and get in the middle of it."

"What happened?"

"Colt laughed it off at first. As far as he was concerned, they were just dating. She was telling people that they lived together; he said she stayed over a lot. Then Cara started getting a little psycho, and he broke things off completely." He glanced over at her. "Do you think there's a possibility that someone like that might just possibly have taken matters into her own hands to make sure that Colt didn't know you wanted to get back together?"

Cassie nodded slowly. She was having a hard time processing what he'd told her. "Yes. I do. It sounds like a distinct possibility. What do I do?"

Pete smiled. "What you should have done in the first place. Talk to him. Face to face."

"I should. I will." Even to herself, her voice sounded shaky. "But maybe it's too late? This morning I told him that the only thing left for us to say was goodbye … and he said goodbye."

"So? I think he'd still do or say anything you told him to." They were up on the north shore now, almost to her house. "Call him, Cassie. Set up a time to talk to him and set things straight between you once and for all."

"Yeah."

Pete pulled into her driveway. "Call him tonight?"

"No! I need to wrap my head around it first, but I will. Thanks, Pete."

"Anytime. I just wished we'd talked about this sooner. Mind if I ask you something?"

"What?"

"Why have you been so mad at him since you came back?"

"I know I must have seemed pretty childish, and I suppose it was. But not in the way you think. I wasn't mad at him at all."

"So why refuse to even talk to him?"

She gave him a sad smile. "Because I didn't trust myself to be around him. I didn't want to cry or say anything to let him know that I still wish … I thought he was done with me."

"But you knew he wasn't with Cara anymore."

"Yes, but just because he wasn't with her didn't mean he'd ever consider being with me again."

"Well, if I were you, I'd talk to him sooner rather than later. You two have lost enough time."

"Thanks, Pete." She went to open the door.

"I'm serious, Cass. Don't waste any more time." He held her gaze for a moment. "If you don't talk to him about it soon, I will. "

She stared back at him. "You don't need to do that."

He smiled. "I hope not."

Colt checked the clock on the wall. His shift was almost over, and for once, he had the whole weekend off. He was looking forward to it. Not that he had any big plans. He needed to clean the house and catch up on his chores and go grocery shopping. He made a face. Didn't he lead an exciting life?! At least he was going out on Saturday night. That was something to look forward to. Summer Lake might be a backwater; it wasn't the kind of place where someone in law enforcement was ever likely to lead an exciting life, but it was interesting.

He'd bet that most small-town deputies would trade with him if given the chance. The community he served included a big-name country music star, Clay McAdam, who sang at the resort sometimes. There were a bunch of multi-millionaires, Colt suspected possibly billionaires, who lived around the lake. They had security teams whom he kept in touch with. Life was good, if mostly uneventful, and he knew it.

He looked at the clock again. Paperwork was never his favorite aspect of the job, and he couldn't wait to get finished.

"You look like a kid waiting for the bell to ring on a Friday afternoon."

He smiled at Don, the sheriff.

"What's up? You got a hot date tonight or something?"

Colt made a face. "Err, no."

"You should. You need to find yourself a girl and settle down. I had high hopes when Cassie came home."

Colt didn't say anything. He wasn't about to tell Don that he'd had high hopes too—or that she'd dashed any hope he had just a few days ago.

"You should ask her out. Put your pride away."

He let out a short laugh. He'd never had any pride when it came to Cassie. He would have done anything for her. He'd waited for her for years. He'd refused to give up when she chose her career over him. He'd understood that she had to do what she had to do. Even when she'd come back and refused to even talk to him, he'd hung in there—clinging to the belief that one day she'd get over whatever she was so mad about. But on Monday morning, she'd finally gotten through to him. She'd asked him to say goodbye. And he had.

Don was watching him. "Are you thinking about it?"

"About …?"

"Doing what I say. Asking her out."

"No. I'm wishing that it was still possible. But she's made clear, it's over for good."

"I'm sorry to hear that, son."

"Thanks."

"Maybe you should use your weekend off to find a sweet little thing to help you put it behind you?"

"Maybe you're right. Maybe I should."

"Go on. Get out of here. Make the most of your weekend."

"Thanks. I will. You have a good weekend, too."

Don grinned. "I plan to. I'll be here while Mary's family's in town."

Colt laughed. "You're so bad."

"Nah, she understands. It works out best for everyone. They sit and talk. I get to catch up on my paperwork in peace."

Colt grabbed his jacket and shrugged into it. "See you Monday."

"Yeah. See ya."

Colt stopped at the grocery store on the way home. He'd eaten out every night this week because he hadn't wanted to sit home feeling sorry for himself. It was time to get himself back on track. He'd managed for the last several years to live a normal life without Cassie. Now he had to get back into that routine. Nothing had really changed since they talked on Monday. At least, nothing real. The only thing that had happened was that she'd taken away his hope. He needed to pull himself together, needed to somehow see it as a good thing. In a way, she'd set him free. He'd never felt truly free to look for someone new, to consider the possibility of starting a life with anyone who wasn't her. Now he knew that was exactly what he had to do. If he wanted a life—and he did, he wanted to have kids someday—then he needed to find someone to share it with.

"Hey, Colt."

He smiled at Shayna, who was working the cash register. "Hi."

"Are you working this weekend?"

"No. I have both days off for once."

"Oh, that's good."

"It is."

Her cheeks turned pink as she smiled at him, and he had a feeling he knew what was coming next. "Are you doing anything tomorrow night?"

He shrugged. He didn't want to tell her he was going to the Boathouse, didn't want her to say that she'd be there, too. She was nice enough, but …

"See, I was wondering …" Her cheeks were bright red now. "I heard Clay McAdam's going to be singing with the band, and I'd love to go. Do you … would you … Do you want to go with me?"

He stared at her for a moment. He didn't want to go with her. She was a nice enough person. She was good-looking. He let his gaze travel over her. Hot might be a better word. Why had he never noticed that before? He knew the answer. It was because he didn't usually look at women in that way. All he usually noticed was that they weren't Cassie. He nodded, more to himself than to her. He and Cassie were history. She'd made that clear. Shayna might not be someone he saw himself finding a future with, but he wouldn't know for sure unless he got to know her.

She smiled cautiously, and he realized that she'd taken his nod as a yes. He felt bad. He could hardly change his yes to a no now. He smiled back at her.

"Sure. We could do that."

"Oh! Great! That's great!"

Colt looked over his shoulder when someone started to put their groceries on the conveyor behind him. Then he looked back at Shayna. "I'll pick you up at eight."

"Awesome!" She was thrilled.

Colt picked up his bags and smiled at her as he left. When he reached his car, he threw the bags in the trunk. What had he done? He didn't want to go out with Shayna. He wanted to hang out with the guys. Catch up with his friends. Why in hell's name had he said yes? He didn't know. But he did know it was too late to change his mind now. He'd go out with her this once. Then he'd let her down gently afterward. He'd had enough practice at doing that over the last few years.

Chapter Three

Cassie checked herself over in the mirror and nodded. She looked good. Her long brown hair hung loose around her shoulders. She'd thought the dress might be too much—she usually wore jeans when she went to the Boathouse. It wasn't a dressy place. But tonight was a big deal. Clay McAdam was singing, and rumor had it that some of his friends might be there, too. Lawrence Fuller and Shawnee Reynolds had been spotted around town on occasion and Matt McConnell and his fiancée Autumn Breese showed up at the Boathouse quite regularly.

She wasn't wearing a dress because of a bunch of country singers, though. She was wearing it because Colt always used to love this color on her. And he was a sucker for a girl in a dress. He always had been. Memories flashed through her mind. How many times had he pushed her dress up around her waist so he could make love to her? She closed her eyes as a shiver ran down her spine. So many times, but perhaps not as many as the number of times she'd thought about it in the years they'd been apart.

She turned and went back downstairs. Would tonight mark the beginning of more years together? She hoped so. But she was nervous. She should have called him on Monday like Pete had told her to. Instead, she'd tormented herself all week.

She'd picked up the phone a dozen times but chickened out. She hoped that Pete was right. That Colt still wanted to be with her. That Cara had intercepted the message she'd left asking if he wanted to get back together—and that he knew nothing about it.

She picked up her phone from the counter in the kitchen. She could call him now—ask if he was going to be there tonight. She was assuming he would, but it wouldn't hurt to check. She set the phone back down. He'd be there. Hopefully, he'd be willing to hear her out. She wrung her hands together. She felt like such an idiot when it came to Colt. In the rest of her life, she had everything together. She'd pursued the career she wanted, gone to medical school, survived her residency. She'd had friends in the city—as many as her job allowed. A nice apartment. A good life. A healthy bank account.

When her parents had announced their plans to sell this house, it'd shaken her to her core. She'd grown up here. She might not have been back in years, but she loved this place. Her parents had moved to the Bay area years ago. It didn't make any sense for them to keep the house anymore; they rarely came up here. But Cassie hated the thought of letting it go. When her parents had come up to put the place on the market, they'd had dinner with their old friends, Lizzie and Doc. Doc had been the only general practitioner at the lake when Cassie was a kid. His son, Michael, had returned from Australia and taken over the practice—and he was looking for a partner. That was how she'd ended up back here. She had a job she loved. She'd bought the house she loved from her parents. She picked the phone up again. Was it too much to ask that she might finally be able to work things out with the man she'd always loved?

She jumped when the phone rang in her hand. She checked the display and saw that it was Pete.

"Hey," she answered.

"Hey, Cass. Are you going into town tonight? Do you want a ride?"

"Thanks, but I'm okay. I'm going to drive myself."

"Why do that? We're going. We can take you and give you a ride home after, too. Or if you want to do your own thing, you can take a cab. You don't have to be stuck with us if you don't want."

Cassie thought about it. The main reason she didn't want to ride with them was because she knew Pete would give her a hard time about not having spoken to Colt yet.

She heard him chuckle. "And if it helps, Holly told me that I'm forbidden to talk to or about Colt without your express permission."

That made her laugh. "Tell her I said thanks."

"You can tell her yourself when we pick you up. How long do you need?"

She looked around. All she needed to do was put her coat on. "I'm ready when you are. Thanks, Pete."

"No problem. We'll see you whenever Holly's ready."

Cassie hung up and went to look out the window at the lake. She loved this view. Especially on nights like tonight. Although it was dark, the moon was already high in the sky and cast a beautiful silver sheen over the surrounding mountains. Ripples sparkled on the lake. It was beautiful. She and Colt had walked down on the beach on many nights like this. He knew how much she loved it. He used to check the almanac, so he knew the phases of the moon. She smiled. He'd always been a thoughtful guy like that.

She pulled herself together and went to fetch her coat from the hall closet. Perhaps tonight would mark a new beginning for them. She was nervous, but the butterflies in her stomach weren't caused by nerves. She was excited, too.

~ ~ ~

Colt pulled up in front of Shayna's place and cut the engine. This was such a bad idea. It wasn't fair to her, and he knew it. He didn't want to go out with her. What he should do was tell her that. But he couldn't make himself do it. He felt bad. He'd spend the evening with her; she was a nice enough girl. The only thing he had against her was that she wasn't Cassie. That and the fact that he'd rather spend an evening with his friends.

He looked up when the light over the porch came on. She must have seen him. He got out of the car and smiled when the front door opened.

"Hey! I wasn't sure if you were waiting for me to come out." She pulled the door closed behind her and fastened her coat before hurrying up the path to meet him.

"No. Sorry. I was just coming."

She smiled. "Are you going to leave your car there? We can walk back here afterward if you want to have a drink."

He got the feeling that she wanted him to understand that she was happy for him to come home with her later. She reached up and kissed his cheek, enveloping him in a spicy perfume that tickled his nose.

He smiled and opened the car door for her. "Thanks, but it's too cold to be walking home. I can drop you off, no problem." It was bad enough that he was taking her out when he didn't want to. He needed to make his intentions—or lack of them— clear. He didn't want to lead her on into thinking that he was interested in taking her to bed.

When they got to the Boathouse and she shrugged out of her coat, he questioned himself. She really was a good-looking woman. Hot was the word. And she was obviously trying to make the most of her assets. She wore a low-cut top that made her breasts look as though they might spill out at any moment.

It was an appealing sight, there was no denying that. But it just made him feel bad again. He didn't know her well, but what he did know of her—and what he'd liked about her—was that she was down-to-earth. A kind soul, not the kind of girl who would wear a top like that. It made him feel bad because he knew she was doing it for his benefit, and he just wasn't interested. Why couldn't he make himself come clean with her? The right thing to do would be to put them both out of their misery.

Instead, he made himself smile at her. "You look great."

"Thank you!"

"What can I get you to drink?"

"Rum and Coke, please. I'll go find us a table."

He watched her walk away. Part of him wished he was the kind of guy who would just take a girl to bed for the fun of it.

"What can I get you, Deputy?"

He turned back to the bar, surprised that Kenzie was there to serve him already. "A rum and Coke and a Coke. Thanks, Kenz."

She gave him a stern look. "The rum and Coke's for Shayna?"

He nodded. It was none of Kenzie's business, but he knew that he was about to get the third degree, nonetheless.

Kenzie frowned at him. "Sorry, bud. But what are you playing at?"

He laughed. "What do you mean?"

"Well, she's not the kind of girl who's into one-nighters. And to be fair, you're not that kind of guy either. But at the same time, I don't see you dating her for real now that Cassie's back in town. Hence the question—what are you playing at?"

He made a face. "The honest answer is, I don't know."

Kenzie held his gaze for a moment then set the drinks on the bar in front of him. "Well, you might want to figure it out.

Shayna's nice. Don't mess her around just because you and Cassie haven't figured things out yet."

Colt scowled at her. "Cassie and I have figured things out. We're over. Done for good." Colt thrust a twenty across the bar at her.

"Oh! Shit. I'm sorry. But still, that's no reason to mess Shayna around."

Colt's anger subsided as fast as it had come. "I know. You're right. I shouldn't have brought her."

Kenzie smiled. "Hey, we all do dumb stuff when it comes to love. For what it's worth, I don't believe you and Cassie are over for good. You wait and see."

Colt shrugged. He wasn't about to explain that he had waited and that now he finally knew. "Thanks, Kenz." He picked up the drinks and let her get on with serving other customers. The bar was already busy, and he didn't need to hold her up.

"Hey, Colt." Logan stepped in front of him as he moved away from the bar.

"Hey."

Logan eyed the drinks in his hands. "That one," he pointed at the Coke, "tells me that you're driving tonight. And that one …" He pointed at the rum and Coke, which was garnished with two slices of lime. He smiled and raised an eyebrow. "That one tells me that you have company this evening."

Colt nodded reluctantly.

"Go on, who's the lucky lady?"

"Logan!" Roxy pushed at his arm and turned to Colt. "Sorry."

"It's okay. He's right." He looked around and spotted Shayna, who was perched at one of the high-top tables. "I'm out with—"

"Shayna!" Logan grinned. "Wow. I don't know about you, but I can tell how she hopes tonight will go. I never knew she had a set—" He stopped abruptly when Roxy slapped his arm hard.

"What?" he asked innocently. "I didn't know she had such a lovely set of earrings." He smirked at Roxy and Colt.

Colt couldn't help but glance to check. It was true. She was wearing long, shiny gold earrings.

Logan laughed. "You were the one who wasn't looking at her earrings."

Roxy rolled her eyes. "And you expect us to believe that's what you were talking about? You're so bad."

"You have to trust me, babe. I only have eyes for you."

"I know! What bothers me is the way you objectify women's bodies. She's a person, not a set of boobs."

Logan shook his head at Colt. "Apparently, I'm just a caveman."

Colt smiled. "You were, but Roxy has you halfway reformed already."

"Are you going to bring her over to sit with everyone?" asked Roxy. "Angel and Luke have snagged us a table near the dance floor."

"No." Much as he'd like to spend the evening with his friends, he didn't want to bring Shayna to join them. He didn't want to give her or them the idea that tonight was anything more than a one-off.

Logan understood his reasoning immediately, but Roxy frowned.

"What's up?" he asked.

"Is it because Cassie's coming?"

Colt's heart slammed to a halt. He'd hoped she wouldn't be here tonight. But he'd told himself that if she were, him being with Shayna would send her the right message; he understood that they were over, and he was moving on.

Logan raised an eyebrow at him.

"It has nothing to do with Cassie. I didn't even know she was coming."

Logan nodded. "And now that you do …?"

He shrugged. "It doesn't make any difference."

Shayna was watching them and gave him a little wave.

"I should get over there, not leave her sitting by herself."

"Okay, we'll catch up with you later."

Colt nodded and made his way to where Shayna was sitting. Just before he reached her, he glanced over at the big table where more of his friends had now gathered. Logan pointed over, and they all looked at Shayna. None of them looked too happy about it, but to his surprise, Abbie looked really pissed. He blew out a sigh. It had nothing to do with her—or any of them, for that matter.

He set the drinks down on the table and smiled at Shayna, determined to make this at least a pleasant evening for her. It wasn't her fault that his friends thought he should be with Cassie. And to be fair, it wasn't their fault that they didn't know what Cassie had told him—that it was over.

"Did you used to date Abbie or something?" Shayna asked when he sat down.

"No, why?"

"Because I saw all your friends talking about you being here with me, and she looks mad as hell about it."

He shrugged. "Sorry. I saw that, too. I don't know what her problem is."

"She works with Cassie, doesn't she?"

Jesus! He was starting to wonder if he'd ever get to have another conversation in his life where Cassie's name didn't come up. "Yeah."

Shayna smiled sadly. "I knew it was stupid of me to ask you out. You're still not over her, are you?"

He stared at her for a long moment, his mind racing. "No." That was the truth, and Shayna didn't need to know the rest— that Cassie, apparently, was over him.

"Yeah. I think I knew that, but I hoped."

He gave her an apologetic smile. "I'm sorry. I do like you. But …"

"I know. It's okay. Do you want to call it a night?"

"No! Please stay? We can hang out, can't we? I'd hate for you to go home now."

"Sure. If you want a friend, I'm happy to be one. But don't you have a whole bunch of friends over there?"

"I do. But …" His heart leaped into his throat when he saw Cassie come in with Pete and Holly. He could feel the blood rushing to his temples—and to the front of his pants. Damn! He'd always loved her in a dress. There was nothing about the one she was wearing that should affect his body like this. It wasn't particularly short. It didn't showcase her breasts, like Shayna's top did. There was nothing revealing about it at all. Nothing except the way it showed off her gorgeous figure—or the memories it brought back of him pushing her skirt up around her waist when he was in so much of a hurry to be inside her that they couldn't wait to undress.

Shayna followed his gaze. "Are you sure you want me to stay?"

He had to drag his eyes away from Cassie to look at her. He didn't know what to say.

"Seriously." Pete fixed Holly with a determined look. "Give me one good reason why I shouldn't go and talk to Colt the minute I see him. Cassie's been putting it off all week. You know I don't like delays. I like to see things resolved."

Cassie sucked in a deep breath. Pete and Holly had been discussing her as if she weren't there for most of the ride into town. She appreciated that they cared about her—Pete wanted to straighten things out for her, and Holly wanted him to respect her right to go about things in her own way. But they were so caught up in it they seemed to have forgotten about her and what she might want.

She looked around, hoping to see the rest of the gang. Hoping that once they met up with the rest of their friends, Pete and Holly would leave her alone. As she scanned the room, she froze when she saw him. He'd been good-looking when they were kids, but now that he was older, he was even more so. His shoulders had filled out, there were a few streaks of silver at his temples. He made her heart race. He was sitting at one of the high-top tables. She couldn't figure out who was sitting with him.

"There they are." Holly slipped her arm through hers and started leading her toward the dance floor.

Cassie looked back at Colt and then turned to see the whole gang seated beside the dance floor. Her heart raced. He wasn't with them? Then who was he with?

When they reached the table, Abbie gave her a look she didn't understand. It was part anger, part sympathy.

"Where's Colt?" Pete asked of no one in particular and everyone in general.

Cassie's heart sank at the way everyone went quiet, and some of them looked away.

Abbie came over to her. She was the only one who knew. She'd been there for her on Monday morning when she'd cried. And she'd been supportive ever since.

"It's okay. I saw him," Cassie told her.

"Saw what?" asked Pete.

Abbie made a face at him. "Colt's out with Shayna tonight."

"What the fuck?" Pete looked pissed.

Cassie forced herself to laugh. It was ironic, if not funny. She'd finally gotten herself together enough to tell him how she really felt, just at the same time as Colt had finally found it within him to move on. She looked around at them and shrugged. "What did I expect? I couldn't ask the poor guy to wait for me forever, could I?"

Chapter Four

Shayna put her hand on top of Colt's, bringing him back to the present and making him jump. "I'm going to leave you to it," she said with a sad smile.

He felt bad. "I'm sorry. I shouldn't have asked you out tonight."

She squeezed his hand. "You didn't, remember? I asked you. I knew you and Cassie had a lot of history, but I thought maybe it was behind you."

"It is. At least, as far as she's concerned, it is. I know I need to put it in the past, but I guess I'm not quite there yet. I'm sorry. Let me drive you home?"

"No. I'd guess by the way Cassie keeps looking at you, she might not be as over it as you think. You should talk to her."

Colt glanced over. Cassie had her back to him, talking to Abbie. Abbie gave him a look that made him glad she was on the other side of the room.

Shayna slid down from her stool. "I'm not going home. Some of my girlfriends are here, and I want to hear Clay sing anyway."

Colt got to his feet. "I'm sorry, Shayna."

She smiled. "Don't be. I hope you and Cassie can work it out." She reached up and put her arms around his neck to kiss his cheek.

Of course, Cassie chose that moment to look over at them. Colt's heart raced in his chest. He didn't want her to see him hugging another girl. Even if he knew she didn't care.

"You take care, Colt."

"You, too." He watched Shayna go over to a table full of girls on the other side of the dance floor. He watched as she chatted with them and sat down, imagining what the conversation might be. He felt like an asshole. He shouldn't have done that to her.

He sat there sipping his beer. He could hardly go and join the gang now. Maybe it'd be better for everyone if he just went home. He glanced over at Cassie. He didn't want to leave. She might not want to be with him, but even getting to watch her was better than nothing.

Ivan was standing beside her and caught his eye and gave him a look he couldn't decipher. Maybe he knew what Abbie's problem was. It seemed he was about to find out.

Ivan made his way over and pulled up the seat Shayna had just left. "Want to tell me what's going on?"

Colt laughed. "You mean, do I want to admit what a total idiot I am? Not sure I do, thanks. No."

Ivan smiled. "Try me. When we had dinner the other night, you said that you might bend my ear one day soon. I'd guess tonight might be the night since you just had a pretty girl leave you sitting here alone, and you're not coming to join everyone. Want to tell me what that's about?"

Colt blew out a sigh. "It's about Cassie. It seems like, for me, everything is always about Cassie, even now."

"You still like her?"

Colt laughed. "I thought you were supposed to be a smart guy? Of course, I do. The trouble is, she doesn't want anything to do with me anymore."

Ivan frowned.

"What?"

"I thought you were the one who didn't want anything to do with her?"

"What the hell gave you that idea?"

"Abbie did. She was all worked up about how upset Cassie was. About how Cassie's such a mess because you don't want to be with her anymore."

"She's got the wrong end of the stick there. Cassie doesn't want to be with me."

Ivan's frown grew deeper. "It sounds to me like someone has the wrong end of the stick, but I don't think it's Abbie. Why don't you talk to Cassie?"

"Because she made it clear that we have nothing left to say."

They both looked up when Pete set three beers down on the table. "S'up, guys?"

Colt shook his head. "Nothing."

Pete fixed him with a hard stare. "Try again."

Colt had to laugh. "I've always wished I could master that look. I could interrogate anyone if I could do that."

Pete didn't smile. "What's going on with you?"

"What do you mean?"

"I mean, Cassie's finally figured out what went wrong between you guys, and you're here screwing things up by being out with Shayna."

Colt bristled at that. He was getting a bit sick of everyone feeling as though they got a say in his life. "First of all, it's none of your goddamned business. And how am I screwing anything up? Cassie doesn't want to be with me, so ... what? I can never date anyone else again?"

"Cassie does want to be with you, idiot! She was going to tell you that tonight."

Colt stared at him. "What?"

"You heard me."

Colt had heard, but he wasn't sure he believed. He glanced over at Cassie. For the first time tonight, she met his gaze and gave him a look that melted his heart. She looked sad and scared, and all he wanted to do was to make her feel better.

Pete put a hand on his shoulder. "I know it's none of my goddamned business, bro. But I'm not going to apologize. I'd like to bang your heads together, but instead, I'm going to suggest that you go get her, take her out of here, take her home, or anywhere but here. And talk to her. Talk until you're both straight about what happened between you and about how you both feel."

Colt looked up at him. Part of him wanted to tell him to butt out, but another, bigger part of him, wanted to take his advice. He glanced at Ivan, who smiled.

"Do it. I have a feeling that right now, you'd like to punch him, but if you do as he says, then by tomorrow, you'll want to thank him."

Pete grinned. "Just go. If you still want to punch me tomorrow, you can. How about that?"

Colt nodded. His heart was racing as he got to his feet. If it were anyone else, he would have told them where they could shove their advice. His heart had taken enough of a battering this week. But Pete wasn't one to interfere, normally. And he wasn't one to get things wrong. He knew something that Colt didn't. And Colt knew he'd have to talk to Cassie to find out what it was.

~ ~ ~

Cassie's heart raced as she watched Colt make his way toward her. There was no doubt in her mind that Pete had just told him that he needed to sort things out with her. For all that she'd begged Pete not to interfere, right now, she was grateful that he had. She'd handled things so poorly herself.

She didn't know how this was going to go, but for the first time in years, she had hope that things between her and Colt might work out. Before he'd said goodbye to her on Monday morning, he'd told her that there were still so many things he wanted to say to her. There were so many things she wanted to say to him, too. And now she finally understood that he might want to hear them.

Her breath caught somewhere in her throat when he reached her. For the longest moment, they stood there, looking into each other's eyes. It felt as though the busy bar around them melted away. It was just the two of them again.

Eventually, he smiled. "It sounds like we need to talk."

She nodded, unable to make her voice work.

"Do you want to get out of here?"

She nodded again. She might not be able to form words, but she wanted to reassure him. She reached for his hand and turned for the door.

She was aware of everyone watching them as they left. She felt as though every single pair of eyes in the place was on them. When they finally made it out through the main doors, she let out a big breath.

Colt squeezed her hand. "Are you okay?"

She looked up into his eyes. His beautiful brown eyes that she'd loved for so long. "Yeah. Better now that we're out of there." She shivered and realized that she hadn't even stopped for her coat.

He smiled, and she knew that he understood. "The way I see it, we have two choices. Either we can go back in there for our coats, or we can freeze our asses off till we get to the car."

She smiled back. "I don't want to go back in."

"Good. Me neither. Is your car here?"

"No."

"That's okay. I have the truck."

They hurried across the parking lot, and he opened the door for her before he ran around to the driver's side and got in. He started the engine and turned the heater on. "This thing warms up quickly."

"Good. I'm frozen already."

"Do you want to go to my place?"

She met his gaze. She could hardly tell him that she'd love to!

His expression changed. "Sorry. I only meant because it's warm. I'm not ... I know you don't want ..." He looked so damned uncomfortable.

She couldn't help it. She reached across and touched his cheek. "That's the trouble, Colt. It's been the trouble all along. I do want."

He stared at her for a long moment. "You do?"

She nodded.

He put the truck in gear and backed out. She knew by the expression on his face that he wanted, too. This might not be the best idea, but it was all she could think about. They'd always been so good together in bed. They might have messed up the other aspects of their relationship, but in bed, there'd never been any question that they were perfect for each other.

When they reached his place, he drove straight into the garage. Cassie got out and came around to meet him at the door that led into the kitchen. It might have been years since she'd been here, but it felt so familiar—so right.

The garage door slid shut. And Colt looked back at it before coming to stand before her. "Do you want to talk?"

She nodded reluctantly. Back in the parking lot, she'd been overcome with desire. All she'd wanted was to be with him again. To feel his naked body against hers. To … She had to stop this! They needed to talk things through. There was so much she had to explain. So much she needed him to explain.

His gaze traveled over her body, eliciting the same reaction as if he'd touched her with his hands. "I thought we were done?"

She shook her head. "I thought you didn't want me."

His head jerked up as if she'd slapped him. "Why? I've always loved you. I never stopped telling you that. You chose your career. That hurt, but I respected it. I still loved you. I still always hoped."

Cassie felt a tear escape. "You never got my message, did you?" She knew now that he hadn't.

"What message?"

"When you were with Cara."

He flinched.

"I called you to ask if you could forgive me; if you'd take me back. I left a message. She called me back and said that you'd asked her to. That you didn't want to talk to me, but you needed me to know."

She watched his face as he processed what she'd said. He closed his eyes, but she could still see the pain. "Jesus!" He threw his head back.

She nodded. "That's why I was so mean to you when I came back. All I wanted was for us to get back together, but I knew—at least I thought I did—that you were done with me. Over us. I just didn't know how to be around you but not with you. All I could think of was to avoid you—for both our sakes.

I didn't want to embarrass you, and I didn't want to put myself through that kind of hurt."

He stepped toward her. "Cassie, I would have taken you back any day, any time. If I'd known ..." He shook his head. "I can't believe she did that."

Cassie touched his cheek, and he looked down into her eyes. "Do you want me back?"

He nodded and put his hands on her hips, pulling her toward him. "I do. Do you still want me?"

She nodded but didn't get the chance to speak before his lips came down on hers.

It had been years since they last kissed, but it felt like no time at all. His lips were familiar still. The way they crushed against hers, the way his tongue slid inside her mouth. She clung to his shoulders and kissed him back. For so long, she'd believed that she'd never get to kiss him again. Now the moment was here, she couldn't get enough of him. He pulled her closer against him. It was all so familiar and yet different. He was bigger, more solid. His arms were more muscular, his chest hard as her breasts pushed up against it.

They were both breathing hard when he lifted his head. "Do you want to come in?"

She nodded and followed him into the kitchen. She almost bumped into the back of him when he stopped abruptly. "What's wrong?"

He turned around and took her face between his hands. "I've dreamed about this moment, Cass. So many times. I've pictured you back here with me. I've thought about you back in my life, in my arms." He raised an eyebrow. "In my bed?"

She smiled. "If you're asking if I'm sure, I'm sure."

"Do you think we need to talk first?"

She shook her head and moved her hands over his chest, searching for buttons that would let her inside. "No. I don't.

We can talk later. I've dreamed about this moment, too. I want it. I want you, Colt."

She closed her eyes as he reached down and slid his hands up her thighs. "You know what I was thinking when I saw you in a dress tonight, right?"

"I hoped." She breathed. "I hoped that you'd remember …" She gasped as his fingers found their way inside her panties. She was already wet for him. She reached for his zipper, but he moved his hips away.

He walked her backward into the living room, and she closed her arms around his neck, trusting him completely that he wouldn't let her fall.

"We should take it upstairs," he breathed.

"We'd never make it." This time he didn't stop her when she reached for his zipper and pushed his jeans and boxers down. She closed her fingers around him and watched him suck in a deep breath.

"You're right." He pulled her down on the sofa beside him and claimed her mouth in a kiss. She gave herself up to him, knowing that he would soon claim her body in the same way.

Her skirt was up around her waist, and her panties were gone. She reached for him and he bit down on her neck as she worked her hand up and down his length. He was so hot and hard; she couldn't wait to feel him inside her. She maneuvered herself underneath him and spread her legs.

He held her gaze as he positioned himself above her. "I've missed you so much, Cassie."

She nodded and closed her hands around his ass. "I've missed you, Colt. I need you back."

He thrust his hips, and they both gasped as he buried himself deep inside her. He felt so good, so right. They moved together frantically, their bodies remembering the rhythm that had made them one all those years ago.

She wrapped her arms around his neck and pulled him down to kiss her. She'd always loved the way their mouths fit together in the same way their bodies did. He filled her, stole her senses, and carried her higher and higher on a wave of pleasure that was building inside her. He was getting closer with each thrust; she felt him tense and then he let go. His release triggered hers and she cried his name as her orgasm tore through her. She felt as though they were soaring away. He was taking her back to a place where only the two of them existed, a place she hadn't been in all the years they'd been apart.

When they finally stilled, he lifted his head and looked down into her eyes. "I love you, Cassie. I never stopped loving you."

She felt tears prick her eyes. Lying here like this with him, it seemed crazy to her that she could ever have doubted. Of course, he loved her. Just as she loved him. "I never stopped loving you."

He dropped a kiss on her lips. "Never?"

She shook her head. "I thought I made the right choice—for both of us. I thought you'd hate the life I needed to live. I still think you would have. But …"

He traced his finger over her lips. "None of it matters anymore, does it?"

She looked into his eyes and smiled when she realized that he was right. "It really doesn't, does it? We can't change what happened, but we can decide where we go from here. We can make the right choices this time."

He smiled. "We can. I'm not sure that jumping your bones the minute I got you back to my place was necessarily the right choice, but I can't say that it was a bad one."

She laughed. "It was the perfect choice. We were always good at this. We never had misunderstandings in bed."

"Yeah, I could always show you how much I loved you, even when I didn't get the words right."

"Exactly. I'm sure there are still a lot of words we need to say, but now we're relaxed and comfortable with each other first."

He rolled off her and kneeled beside the sofa. "I'm definitely relaxed, but we should clean up before I can say I'm truly comfortable."

Chapter Five

Colt splashed water over his face and then looked himself in the eye in the mirror. Tonight couldn't have turned out more differently than he'd expected. Instead of dropping Shayna off at her place, he'd brought Cassie back to his place—and made love to her!

He shook his head in wonder. He'd been overtaken with desire for her. It'd taken every drop of willpower he possessed not to take her up against the wall in the garage. They hadn't made it as far as the bedroom, but still … maybe they would later.

He dried his face and tried to wrap his head around what she'd told him. She'd wanted to get back together. She'd called him to ask if he still loved her—and if he'd forgive her. He closed his eyes against the anger that bubbled up inside him.

Cara had been a mistake. A very beautiful, very horny mistake. She'd made a determined play for him, and hey, he was a guy. He could only resist a woman like that for so long. At the time, he'd believed that Cassie wanted him to find someone else and move on with his life. She knew he wanted to have kids someday, that he wanted a wife and a family. She'd chosen her career instead. Sure, there were doctors who married and had kids, but Cassie didn't like to do things by half measures. She wanted to throw herself into her career, and that didn't involve coming back to the lake—or getting married—in the foreseeable future.

Cara, on the other hand? Cara had made it plain that she wanted him to marry her. She wanted to have his babies and live here in his house and put up a white picket fence. He shuddered at the memory of coming home to find the changes she'd made to the place—the chintz curtains, the fluffy throw pillows on the sofa. If he was honest, he'd made the same mistake with her as he'd made with Shayna this evening. He'd gotten himself involved in something that he didn't really want and had waited too long to be honest about it. By the time he'd been honest with Cara, she was already too deeply invested. She'd been telling the whole town they were getting engaged.

He wondered if she'd started with that before or after she'd picked up Cassie's message. He couldn't believe that she was so messed up that she'd called Cassie back—and told her that he'd asked her to. That was some kind of crazy.

He heard Cassie moving around downstairs and went back down to find her. Cara may have cost them a few years, but he hoped that nothing could stop them from being together in the end. He finally had another chance, he wanted to make it work. But he wasn't a fool. All the reasons Cassie had for leaving him when they were younger hadn't just evaporated. He still wanted kids. He wanted to raise a family here at the lake. He didn't know how she felt about that now. Granted, she'd come back here, but he couldn't just assume anything. They needed to talk—and there was a lot to talk about.

He found her in the kitchen, sitting on a stool at the island. He went to her and cupped her face between his hands. "For a minute there, I thought I heard you sneaking out of here."

She smiled. "Nope. I don't plan on going anywhere. And even if I did, you'd have to take me. I don't have my car, remember?"

"Oh, that's right." He gave her a sly smile. "So, I can keep you here as long as I like?"

"It looks that way. How long do you want me?"

His first thought was to tell her that he wanted to keep her forever, but he didn't dare go there yet. Instead, he decided to take a chance on something a little more immediate. He raised an eyebrow at her. "That's a whole big conversation, but for starters, can I at least keep you until tomorrow?"

He felt himself relax when she smiled. "I was hoping you might say that."

"I think you know what I really wanted to say."

She nodded and gave him a half smile. "Yeah. I feel that way, too. But there's no rush, right? Forever takes a while."

He had to swallow around the lump that formed in his throat. He'd wondered if she'd even remember about that.

She reached out and squeezed his hand. "I used to tell myself that all the time, you know."

"Me, too. And I'm going to risk saying it, Cass. A while doesn't take forever, either. And we've been apart for a very long while."

She nodded. "You think there might be hope for a forever?"

His heart buzzed in his chest as he closed his arms around her. "I do."

~ ~ ~

Cassie opened her eyes and lay there for a moment, hoping that she wasn't dreaming. If she was, it was the best dream ever. She was in Colt's bed. His arm was snug around her waist, and his head rested against her shoulder.

He nuzzled his lips into her neck. "Are you awake?"

"Mm. Apparently, I am. For a minute there, I wondered if I was dreaming."

He chuckled. "Me, too. I woke up a while ago, and I've just been lying here, trying to convince myself that this is real."

She rolled over and planted a peck on his lips. "I think it's real." She slid her arms around his neck, loving the feel of his warm, hard body against hers. "Do you want to make love to me again quick—just in case we wake up soon and discover it was only a dream?"

He smiled, and his hand closed around her ass, pulling her closer so she could feel how much he liked that idea. "You always were such a smart lady. I think that's an awesome idea."

He rolled onto his back and pulled her with him so that she straddled him. His hand slid between her legs, teasing her until she was moaning with pleasure. He'd always been able to make her come just by touching her—maybe that was because he'd had so much practice at touching when they were young. They'd fooled around for months before they finally made love for the first time.

She rocked her hips in time with him. "You might need to stop that, or you're going to be left out."

He smiled. "I should be a gentleman and take you there first, but ..." He shifted his hips so that his hard cock nudged at her entrance. "I can't wait."

She licked her lips and shook her head. "I don't want you to wait, I want you to ... Yes!" She gasped as he thrust his hips and pulled her down onto him. She closed her eyes and deliberately tightened her muscles around him, wanting to feel him deep.

He grunted and thrust harder, filling her, stretching her, but not yet picking up the pace. She writhed her hips against him, needing more. His hands closed around her ass, spreading her cheeks, opening her up to take him more deeply.

She moaned again and moved with him, wanting to match his slow pace, but soon getting lost in the sensations that rolled through her body. She rested her hands on either side of his head and let her breasts fall in his face. He'd always loved that. She closed her eyes when he took her nipple in his mouth and sucked hard, making her ride him harder. His fingers dug into her ass as he pulled her down to receive his thrusts. He was driving her to the edge, taking her to the point of no return, and when his fingers slid between her cheeks and he touched her there, she screamed and let herself go.

He showed her no mercy; his fingers, lips and hips all worked her frantically until he cried her name and found his release deep inside her. They soared away, back to that place where only they existed. The place she thought that she'd never go again. Just the realization that they now had a future ahead of them sent another rush of pleasure through her.

Finally, she slumped down on his shoulder. They were both breathing hard. His fingers came up and tangled in her hair. "If this is a dream, I don't ever want to wake up."

She lifted her head and looked down into his eyes. "It's not a dream, Colt. It's real. We're getting another chance; we just have to get it right this time."

His eyes clouded over.

"What is it? What's wrong?"

He shook his head and smiled. "Wrong? How could anything be wrong? I have the love of my life back in my bed. She just screwed my brains out, and you think there's something wrong?" He laughed.

She had to smile at the way he'd called her the love of his life, but even after all this time, she knew him too well; something about what she'd said had bothered him. But she didn't need to push it. If it was something important, he'd tell her when he was ready.

"Last night, you asked how long you get to keep me. Do you have any interest in keeping me for the day? Or do you have other plans?"

His arms tightened around her. "I want to keep you for the day." He smiled. "And when this evening rolls around, I'll figure out how I can keep you for the night again, too."

She smiled. "I like the sound of that. The only thing I need to do is get clean clothes." She glanced over at where her dress lay on the floor where he'd thrown it when they came up here last night.

He gave her a sly smile. "Maybe I should just keep you here—naked?"

She laughed. "That'd work, too. But not if you want to keep me for the night. See, I'll have to have clothes to go to work in tomorrow."

He nodded and rolled to his side, sending her sliding down onto the bed. "You're right, of course. What do you say, do you want to join me in the shower, and then you can borrow some sweats to go over to your place?"

She felt as though his mood had shifted. Was it because she'd talked about having to go to work? Her career had been the thing that had come between them—the reason they hadn't stayed together. Did she need to be more careful talking about it? She frowned. No! If they were going to get back together and be able to make a life together, they needed to talk.

He got out of bed, and she sat up, pulling the sheet up around her. "Don't tell me there's nothing wrong again. What did I say?"

She watched the struggle on his face. After a moment, he blew out a sigh. "I didn't want to go there yet." He gave her a rueful smile. "I know there's a lot we need to talk about, but I just wanted to have a little bit of a honeymoon phase before we have to get into the serious stuff."

"Sorry. I'm not trying to get all serious on you. I just don't like it when I know something bothers you—and I like it even less when you won't talk about it. If we're going to make things work this time, we need to be open with each other."

He nodded and sat back down on the bed beside her. He slung his arm around her shoulders and landed a peck on her lips. "I know. But when we go there, we can't take it back."

She frowned. "Take what back?"

He held her gaze for a long moment. "If we were to talk about where we go from here. If I were to want certain things, and if you didn't, well ..." He shrugged. "I hope it's not the case, but there's a chance that we each want very different things out of life. And if we do, then ..." He swallowed. "Then it wouldn't be right for either of us to compromise that much. I guess I'm scared to talk about it because if that's the case, I'd rather not know yet. I just got you back, Cass. I can't say goodbye again."

She wrapped her arms around him and hugged him close. "Colt, please! No. Don't even worry about that. I know—I've always known what you want out of life. That's why I said goodbye because I didn't know for sure that I could give it to you. I know you want a family. You want to have kids and you want to be married—and you don't ever want to leave this place. I know it. Do you really think I could have come back here with you last night, that I would have started things back up if I wasn't ready to say that that's what I want, too?"

His head jerked up, and he met her gaze. "You do?"

She smiled. "I do. I did what I needed to do. I trained. I did my residency, and I've found my perfect job. I thought maybe I wanted something high-powered and intense, but that's not me. I'm much happier back here. It might not be so glamorous, but I know I'm an important part of this town. That what I do makes a difference. That's all I ever wanted—to make a difference, to contribute."

He searched her face.

"I know you're wondering about the rest, too. I always wanted to have kids someday. It just wasn't fair to you to ask you to wait until I figured out when that day might be. You were ready then. I didn't know how long it would take for me."

She watched a little pulse in his temple and saw him swallow. "I wasn't ready for any of it—I didn't want it—without you."

She wiped a tear away. "I'm sorry. I made a mistake. I realized it years ago. I wanted to make it right, but …"

He looked angry. "But Cara screwed that up for us. She cost us years that we could have been together."

Cassie shrugged. "We can't change the past; we can't go through life looking in the rearview mirror."

He smiled. "Maybe that wouldn't be such a bad thing—that way, you'd know when there was a cop following you."

She chuckled. "I'd rather keep this cop in front of me where I can see him."

He got up and reached for her hand. "Want to keep him in front of you in the shower? That way, you'll be able to see what he's doing."

She got to her feet. "What does he plan on doing?"

He smirked. "You'll have to come with me to find out."

~ ~ ~

When he brought the truck to a stop outside Cassie's place, Colt looked around him and sucked in a deep breath.

She looked over at him. "Is it weird to be back here?"

He smiled. "Yeah. It is. I mean, you can never say never, but I didn't think I'd come back here." He reached for her hand

and squeezed it. "Not with you. I saw your folks when they came up. When they were getting ready to put the place on the market."

"They told me. They still love you, you know."

He nodded. "They were always good to me."

"Because they knew you were good to me—that you're good for me."

He cocked his head to one side. "I thought they'd be pleased that you shook off the small-town kid and went out to do great things in the world." He knew that her parents had wanted her to go to medical school. He'd thought that they'd be pleased when she decided not to come back here.

She held his gaze for a moment. "They were sad when I ended things with you. They didn't understand why you wouldn't want to leave here."

He nodded. "This was just one of the places they lived in their lives, though, wasn't it? They don't get that my family's been here for generations."

"No. They don't know what that's like. We stayed here for my high school years, and that was the longest that we ever lived anywhere. Anyway, let's go in."

He followed her into the house and let out a low whistle when she let them inside. "Wow! The place has changed."

She smiled. "Do you like it?"

"I do. It's more modern. It feels more like …" He searched for the right word, then smiled when he found it. "It feels like you."

"Thank you. That's exactly what I was aiming for. When they said they wanted to sell the place, it broke my heart. This house was my last connection to you. I still wasn't ready to let go. When they told me that Michael was looking for a partner, I thought I was crazy at first, even considering coming back here. But the more I thought about it, the more I knew it was the right move for me. I knew you didn't want me anymore—"

Hearing her say that sent a dagger through his heart, knowing that she must have felt the same way he did. He pulled her to him and closed his arms around her. "You thought I didn't, but now you know the truth."

She nodded. "I do, and even though I thought I must be crazy to come back here knowing that we wouldn't be together, if I hadn't come back, we wouldn't be." She shuddered. "Can you imagine? If I hadn't come back, we'd probably never have discovered what Cara did. We would have lived our whole lives, each thinking that the other didn't want us anymore."

He shook his head. "I don't want to think about it. That's rearview mirror stuff. It's behind us now."

"You're right. It is." She smiled. "And it isn't even what I was talking about. I got off track, sorry. I was telling you about the house. I wanted it to feel more modern and more like me, so in the time I've been back, I've had all kinds of work done."

"I can see."

She smiled. "I had to keep myself busy somehow while I spent most of my time holed up here, trying not to run into you."

He hugged her closer. "Well, I hope you got the place how you want it because I don't plan to let you stay holed up here anymore—not unless you're inviting me to join you."

"Anytime you like—all the time, if you like."

He smiled; he did like that idea. That was exactly where he was hoping that things would go for them now, but even that raised questions. If they got together for good this time, would she want him to move here with her? Would she be open to coming to his place?

He dropped a kiss on the top of her head. They were all details that they could work out when the time came. For now, he wanted to do what he'd told her this morning—have a little bit of a honeymoon period—a time to just get to know each other again and enjoy each other's company before they started to figure out the big picture.

Chapter Six

Cassie tapped the brakes as she neared the bakery. She was running a few minutes early this morning. She could stop and get donuts for everyone. She smiled to herself. She'd done that last Monday morning. She couldn't have imagined then how much her life would have changed just one week later.

She decided to drive on. If she went into the bakery, Renée and April would no doubt have questions for her. She and Colt hadn't ventured out from her place yesterday, and he'd spent the night with her before leaving early this morning. But she knew what this town was like. News of them leaving the Boathouse together on Saturday night would have spread like wildfire, and everyone would want to know what was going on between them.

Abbie had texted her yesterday to make sure that she was okay and to tell her that she had her coat and would bring it over if she liked. Cassie had asked her to bring it to work and told her in as little detail as possible that she and Colt were getting back together.

She frowned as she pulled into the little staff parking lot behind the medical center. Why did she keep thinking of it that way? That they were getting back together. They *were* back together, weren't they? She nodded to herself. They were.

She got out of the car when Michael pulled up beside her, wondering if he'd heard anything.

"G'morning, darl'." He greeted her with a grin. "You have yourself a good weekend?"

She smiled back. "Yes, thanks. How about you?"

He chuckled. "It was good, but not the kind of good that yours was. You going to tell me all about it?"

"Sure, but why don't we go in? That way, I can tell you and Abbie at the same time. I'm sure she's ready to interrogate me. There's no point repeating myself."

Michael took her arm with a grin and led her inside. "I have a feeling that you're going to be repeating your tale over and over for the next few days. The grapevine's buzzing, and everyone wants to know."

She rolled her eyes. "We need a local newspaper. I could just post an announcement."

Michael laughed. "There's no way they could print gossip fast enough to keep people happy around here. It's all word of mouth, and …" He grinned at Abbie, who was making coffee in the back room. "We want the words straight from Cassie's mouth, don't we, Abbs?"

Abbie grinned at them. "We most certainly do." She picked up a box and flipped the top open. "I brought pastries, and the coffee's almost ready. This morning's meeting is all about you …" She grinned at Cassie. "… and that very sexy sheriff of yours."

Cassie smiled. He was sexy. She's always thought so, and she'd noticed since she came back to town that she wasn't the only one. She saw the appreciative looks women gave him. She could feel a touch of heat in her cheeks as she remembered the ways that he'd shown her just how sexy he could be yesterday. They'd toured the house as she showed him all the changes and improvements she'd made.

He'd given her a wicked grin when she'd shown him her childhood bedroom. It was an office now. They'd never had sex in there when they were kids. They'd mostly made out in his truck—sometimes at his house—but her house had always been off limits because of her parents.

He'd pushed her skirt up around her waist and told her how often he'd thought about making love to her in this room. Wishing that she'd come back and they could finally christen it. She'd apologized that there wasn't even a bed in there anymore, but he hadn't seen that as a problem. He'd taken her on the desk. She closed her eyes as her body remembered.

"Are you okay?"

She felt her cheeks flush. Abbie and Michael were both watching her.

Michael laughed. "She's fine. She's just thinking about him, right?"

She nodded, feeling embarrassed. "I am. He's wonderful. I'm sorry I've been such a pain in the ass about him since I've been back here."

Michael shrugged. "I'm just glad you guys have finally worked it out."

"Me, too," said Abbie. "But, I want to know how you did and I want to know what's going to happen now?"

Cassie smiled at her. "I don't know yet."

Michael frowned. "I thought it'd be a foregone conclusion. We all thought we knew that you two were lined up for a happily ever after years ago … are you saying you still might not be?"

She shook her head slowly. "I'm hoping, but I don't want to get too carried away."

Abbie smiled. "You're too cautious. It sounds to me like you're finally back on track. Relax. Enjoy it."

Cassie nodded. "I'll get there." There was no reason not to. She knew that. Especially after she and Colt had talked yesterday. He had every right to be cautious about what she might want for the future, but she hoped that she'd reassured him that she wanted all the same things he did. She always had, and now she knew that she was ready.

~ ~ ~

Colt brought the patrol car to a halt in front of the trailer house and checked the envelopes attached to his clipboard sitting on the passenger seat. This was one of his least favorite duties. He didn't understand how any man—or woman, for that matter—could walk away from their child. He just couldn't comprehend how you could have a kid and not want to be a part of their life. No matter what the circumstances might be, he didn't get how a person could shirk their financial responsibility to their child.

He selected the envelope he needed and got out of the car. No matter how much he struggled with the concept, he knew that it was a reality—a reality he dealt with far too often. He was here this morning to serve a court order regarding the nonpayment of child support. He knocked on the door and waited.

After a few minutes of knocking and waiting, the guy he was here to see opened the door and eyed him warily. "Colt."

"Randy."

"What's up?"

Colt held out the envelope. "Remember Sophie?"

Randy pursed his lips. "'Course I do. She's my kid."

"That's right. And when you have kids, you have a responsibility to them, don't you agree?"

Randy blew out a sigh. "You know I don't make much. And besides, when I give Kayleen anything, she spends it on herself, not on the kid."

Colt knew he had a point. "I don't make the decisions, Randy. You know that. I just serve the papers."

Randy grunted and took the envelope.

"Are you going to come good?"

Randy shrugged. "I don't have no choice, do I?"

Colt shook his head. As far as he was concerned, little Sophie was the one who didn't have a choice. She didn't get to choose her parents. Didn't have any control over the shitty life she'd been born into. "No. You don't. Get yourself into town and get on it." He turned and started to walk away.

"Would I still have to pay if Child Services took her?"

Colt turned back around with a frown. "What do you mean?"

"I mean if they took her into care. She'd be a ward of the state, right?"

Colt had to bite back his anger. Was this guy seriously saying that he'd rather his daughter was put into care than have to pay anything toward her upbringing himself?

Randy waved a hand at him. "Don't look at me like that. It's Sophie I'm thinking about. Kayleen's going off the rails. The kid might be better somewhere else."

"You're worried about her?"

Randy nodded. "Yeah. I mean, I know I'm no better, but Kayleen … she's running with a new fella. He's an asshole."

"You're hardly likely to think he's a standup kind of guy, are you?"

"No. But it's not that. He's a mean sumbitch."

Colt nodded and walked back toward him. "What's his name?"

Randy shifted from one foot to the other. "Not sure."

"Come on, Randy! I'll look into it. Your name won't come up. I thought you were worried about Sophie?"

"All right. His name's Jimmy Hansen."

Colt's heart sank. He knew the guy well, and he hated the idea of him being around a seven-year-old girl. He blew out a sigh.

"You run across him before?" asked Randy.

"Too many times. I'll look into it."

"Thanks." Randy waved the envelope at him. "I'll go into town tomorrow. See what I can do. But I meant it, Colt. Do you think she'd be okay if child services took her in? I can't. I'm no use to anyone."

Cole couldn't disagree with his last statement. "It's a tough life for a kid. She might get lucky, find a good foster family …"

"That might be the best thing for her."

Colt shook his head. He knew that Randy was probably right. Neither of Sophie's parents was someone he'd choose to raise a child, but it made Colt sad to think that a little girl's best hope in life might be to be taken into the care system.

As he drove back into town, he couldn't help thinking about Sophie. She was a bright kid. He'd met her a few times when he'd been called to her mother's home—usually on a breach of peace call. He'd seen her at the elementary school one time, too, when he'd gone in to give a talk. She was a bright little thing—curious and chatty. He had to wonder how long it'd be before the life she was living would change her.

When he finished making his other calls of the morning— some of them more serious, but none so distasteful to him as his call on Randy—he decided to make a stop on his way back to the office.

Kelly Miles smiled at him when he knocked on her open office door. "Deputy Stevens. To what do I owe the pleasure? Much as it breaks my heart, I know you're not here to ask me out. I hear you've finally got your lady love back?"

Colt smiled. He liked Kelly a lot, and he knew that she wasn't disappointed he wouldn't be asking her out. She was totally devoted to her girlfriend, Marla.

"News sure travels fast around here."

Kelly shrugged. "You know it. In this line of work, I keep my ear to the ground, but your news spread like wildfire already."

"Yeah. I'm happy and hopeful. But speaking of keeping your ear to the ground. What do you know about Kayleen Wilson and Jimmy Hansen?"

Kelly made a face. "Not as much as you do by the sounds of it. What's happened?"

"Nothing … yet. I'd like to make sure it stays that way."

"The school has me on alert about little Sophie."

Colt nodded. "I went out to see Randy this morning."

"What a charming character he is."

"Yeah. Can you believe that he asked me if he'd still have to pay child support if Sophie was taken into care—because that might be the best solution for her?"

Kelly threw back her head and laughed. "I hope you didn't tell him that he and Kayleen would both have to pay?"

"Nope. If they think there's some benefit in it for them, they'll be more amenable."

"Probably. What do you know about Jimmy Hansen?"

"Nothing good."

"Do I need to start—"

Colt held his hand up. "There's nothing official yet. This is just me. I have a hunch. A bad feeling."

"But you can't police what *might* happen, right? Only what has happened?"

"Yeah. Though when it comes to kids …"

"I know. That's why I do this job. Why don't you do whatever it is you do and see what you can dig up, and I'll call the school, schedule a visit. I'm about due a check-in with them on some of the kids, anyway."

"Thanks, Kelly. I'll get back with you."

"You do that. Kayleen's on my shit list as it is. If this Jimmy character tips the balance, I'll be looking for a placement for little Sophie. Though I have to warn you, she'll probably end up out of county."

Colt frowned.

"There's no other family here—at least, none I'd place her with. And we're overloaded. All our foster families have kids placed with them, and there's no waiting list of prospective fosters. We might get lucky if one of the private agencies comes through, but other than that, if Sophie needs out of the family home, it'll probably mean she's out of Summer Lake, too."

"Okay. I'll touch base with you later."

"Sure. Give Cassie my best."

He smiled. "Thanks. I will. Say hi to Marla for me."

~ ~ ~

It'd been a long day, and Cassie was ready to go home and pour herself a glass of wine. She got into her car and pulled her cell phone out of her purse. Colt had said that he'd call her when he got the chance. It was almost seven now and he hadn't called yet. She hoped that she'd see him this evening, but she knew that with his job, anything might have come up.

She tapped out a text.

Hope your day went ok. I'm guessing you're still busy.

I'm about to head home. Come any time if you want spaghetti and wine.

No worries if not but let me know you're safe.

I love you.

She stared at the screen for a few minutes, hoping that he'd answer before she left. If not, she wouldn't be able to see what he said or answer him till she got home.

The screen stared blankly back at her until her stomach rumbled. The longer she sat here, the longer it'd be before she ate. She started the engine and pulled out of the parking lot.

Once she arrived home, she stopped at the end of the driveway to check the mail. She jumped at the sound of a car horn behind her and turned to see a blue BMW.

"Sorry! I didn't mean to startle you." Holly leaned out the window with a smile. "I was just so excited to catch you. Pete's so proud of himself. I warned him not to interfere, and now he's gone all self-righteous and I-told-you-so. You should know that he's claiming that you and Colt are only back together because of him!"

Cassie laughed. "Let him have it. I know what he's like, and to be fair, he might have a point. He figured out in minutes something that I never would have imagined."

Holly's smile faded. "You mean about what Cara did? I can't believe that! What a bitch! She used to work at the salon, and I didn't like her then. But that's all behind you now. I just wanted to stop and tell you how happy I am for you."

"Thanks."

"We said we'd have you over to dinner soon. I hope you'll bring Colt?"

"I'll ask him."

Holly grinned. "I'm sure he'll say yes. Though it might be a while. I'm doing dinner next Thursday, and you're welcome to come if you want—but it's a kiddie night."

"A kiddie night?"

"Yeah. We don't like to go out all the time anymore. We have Noah, and Jack and Em have Isabel. Michael and Megan have little Billy and Ethan. He's much older, but we invite April and Eddie, too, since their boy Marcus is Ethan's best friend." She stopped. "See? I'm rambling about kids already. My point is that it turns into a kind of madhouse. It's a lot of fun—to me. But I don't know how it'd feel when you don't have kids. So, like I say, you're invited if you want to come, and if you don't, I totally understand. I wouldn't if I were in your shoes."

Cassie smiled. "Thanks. Part of me thinks it sounds like fun, part of me wants to run scared. I'll ask Colt, see what he thinks. He loves kids."

"Oh! That's right! He's like the kiddie whisperer! They all love him. Now I want to be selfish and beg you to come. I'll ply you with wine to make up for Colt being surrounded by adoring little people."

"You might have yourself a deal there. I'll let you know what he says."

"Awesome. Anyway, I'll let you go. I'm going into town to have dinner with Emma, Missy, and Laura. Pete's on Noah duty tonight. Hey! Do you want to come?"

"Thanks, but no. It's been a long day, and I'm looking forward to getting my hands on a glass of wine."

"And on Colt?" Holly waggled her eyebrows.

"Maybe. I hope so. He's still working."

"Aww. I'll keep my fingers crossed for you. I couldn't do it—date a cop. I'd be worried sick the whole time."

"He knows how to take care of himself."

"Yeah. See, that part I could go for—that and the handcuffs."

Cassie laughed. "You're terrible. Go on. Get going, or you'll be late. Say hi to the girls for me, and next time let me know when you're going out for dinner with them. I'd like to come."

"I will. That'll be awesome. Emma gets jealous that I get to see you more often since I'm your closest neighbor."

"Oh! But she's only on the other side of you. I should call her."

"Yeah. Do that. She'd love it. Okay. I'm really going this time. See you soon."

Cassie waved as she pulled away, and then drove down the long driveway to the house. When she'd been a kid, Emma's great aunt had owned the only other house up on this part of the north shore. It'd been a shock when she came back to learn that now Emma and her husband Jack lived there with their little girl, and Pete and Holly had bought the land between her place and theirs and had built a gorgeous home. Part of the appeal of moving back here had been that she would have no close neighbors, but she'd discovered that she loved having those guys close by.

She let herself into the house and shrugged out of her coat before setting a pot of water to boil for the pasta. Once that was going, she went through the mail. There was nothing interesting—some junk and a couple of bills. The last thing she came to was a postcard from her old roommate, who was now an ER doctor in San Diego. She turned it over.

A postcard is the correct medium to send a "Wish You Were Here" message, isn't it?

Well, I do. I miss you. Come back to civilization already! Nothing good is going to happen to you up there in the boonies.

Seriously, I hope you're well and happy, girlfriend. I'd say give me a call, but unless you want me to return it at three in the morning, you know we'll never get to actually speak.

Maybe you can write me? There's something quite cathartic about using pen and paper and then doing something so old school as going to the post office to buy stamps.

Get in touch somehow, and let me know how you are?

Hugs!

Zoe oxoxoxo

Cassie smiled to herself as she went to prop the postcard up on the mantel. Zoe had been her best friend all through medical school. They were overdue for a catchup, but it'd probably have to take place over email—or maybe she'd send her a postcard back. Zoe always joked that Cassie was from Bum Fluff, Nowhere. It'd be fun to send her postcards of just how beautiful this place was. It might even encourage her to come visit. No. That wasn't likely. Even if she wanted to, she'd never find the time.

Zoe was living the life that Cassie had thought she wanted. Working eighteen-hour days—for all intents and purposes, she was married to her job. And that was okay for Zoe because she loved it.

Cassie picked her phone up and checked it; no reply from Colt yet. She hadn't been able to commit to that kind of life in the end. She didn't love it enough. The phone started to ring, and she grinned when she saw his name on the screen. In the end, she hadn't been able to commit to the job she'd thought she wanted. But she was ready to commit to the man she'd always known she loved.

"Hi."

"Hey. I'm sorry. It was a rough day."

Her heart sank. He sounded tired. He probably just wanted to go home. "Aww. I'm sorry for you. Are you too tired to come over? It's all right. I understand."

He chuckled. "Err, no. I'm saying sorry I'm so late. Not sorry that I'm not coming. If you still want me?"

She smiled. "I'll always want you."

His voice was low and sexy when he answered. "I might have to ask you to prove that statement to me later."

She laughed. "So, you're not that tired then?"

"I'll never be that tired."

"Good to know. You get yourself over here, and I'll get this spaghetti going."

"Thanks, Cassie. Do you need me to pick anything up?"

"No. When you get here, I'll have everything I need."

"In that case, I'm on my way."

Chapter Seven

Colt closed his arms around Cassie's waist and drew her to him. "I love my job, and I know you love yours, but I wish we didn't have to go in today."

She reached up and planted a peck on his lips. "Me too. I'd love to spend the day together. Are you working over the weekend?"

"Only on Saturday."

"Do you want to come here when you finish? We could sleep in on Sunday morning and have a lazy day together."

He smiled. "I don't know about sleeping in, but I'd be happy to stay in bed all morning."

She tightened her arms around his waist. "That sounds like a plan to me." She checked her watch. "Unfortunately, I need to get going."

"Yeah, me too." He wondered about asking if she'd rather come to his place over the weekend. She'd stayed with him there that first Saturday night, but since then, they'd spent every night here at her place. She was picking her keys up off the counter and slinging her purse over her shoulder. There wasn't time to get into that conversation now.

She raised an eyebrow at him. "Everything okay?"

"Yeah. Let's go." He followed her out to the garage, where his truck was parked next to her car.

He hugged her to him one last time. "Have a good day."

"You, too. Be safe out there, and I'll see you back here tonight."

He nodded and got into the truck. It seemed she was assuming that he would always come here. He didn't mind. He'd go anywhere to be with her. But if they were really going to get back on track—if this was the beginning of their life together, maybe they should talk about where they were going to build that life. He knew she was attached to this place, but … He got in and backed the truck out of the garage so that she could close the door. What did it matter? Sure, he loved his house, but he'd willingly give it up to be with Cassie. He thought about it as he pulled out onto West Shore Road and followed her into town. He supposed that what bothered him was that he didn't want either of them to just assume anything. They needed to talk about what they each wanted.

He smiled to himself as he glanced out at the lake. He was getting ahead of himself. Just a short time ago, he'd still believed that she never even wanted to talk to him again. He needed to be patient. They might have lost a lot of years, but there wasn't any hurry.

His phone rang, and he frowned as he hit the button to answer, wondering why Don needed to talk to him this early.

"What's up, boss?"

"Hey, Colt. Are you almost here?"

"I'm still out on the west shore."

Don chuckled. "I had a feeling you might be. That's why I'm calling, save you coming in, and then having to go back out. Can you stop by and see Max Douglas?"

"Sure, what's up?"

"You know he has those three old Chevys?"

"I do. He's had them for as long as I can remember. I tried to buy the Chevelle from him when I was a kid."

"Yeah. I think half the kids in town have asked if he'd sell it over the years. But it looks like someone didn't want to take no for an answer. It's gone."

"What?"

"You heard me. He went out into his shop this morning, and it's gone."

"Jesus!"

"I don't think he had anything to do with it, and I wish you'd find a different word."

"Sorry." Don was right, he should find a different go-to word. He didn't like to offend anyone, and he forgot sometimes that that word did.

"It doesn't bother me much, but I cringe every time you say it because I can see Mary's face."

Colt laughed. "I'd never say it in front of her."

"You might not mean to, but it's a bad habit you picked up, and habits become automatic, so find a new one."

"Will do." Colt slowed the truck as he approached the turnoff to Max Douglas's house. "I'm almost at Gramps's place now."

Don laughed. "I forgot all you kids called him that."

Colt smiled. "Yeah, that's probably another habit I should try to quit. This is official business. It should be Mr. Douglas."

Don laughed again. "Nah. The beauty of what we do is that we're part of the community. If you still call him Gramps, then don't change that."

"Okay. I'll be in after I've taken his statement. Do you have any ideas on who might have taken it?"

"I do. But I'm not saying anything until you've talked to him. We can compare notes when you get in."

"Okay. I'll see you later."

He brought the truck to a stop in front of Gramps's house and got out. He smiled and held his hands up in the air when the older man appeared on the porch with a shotgun.

"Hey, Gramps. It's me, Colt Stevens."

"Oh." Gramps set the shotgun down and came down the steps with a grim smile. "That was quick. I just got off the phone with Don."

"And he called me straightaway. I was on my way into work and was just passing here anyway."

Gramps frowned. "You taking the pretty way to work these days? Seems to me as this is a long detour from the route between your house and the sheriff's office."

Colt smiled. "I wasn't coming from my house."

Gramps's frown faded into a smile. "That's right! This car business has thrown me off. You and young Cassie got back together." He nodded happily. "I'm glad to hear that, son. I am. Anyway. Do you want some coffee? I'm going to get me a fresh one before we walk over to the shop."

"Thanks, that'd be great." Colt followed him into the house. "Do you know when the car was taken?"

"Not the time, no. But she was there last night. I can't believe I didn't hear a thing. I'd swear I only get a couple hours sleep a night. I spend most of the time lying there thinking—or getting up to pee—but I guess those times I'm asleep, I sleep deep. I didn't hear a damned thing. You could have knocked me down with a feather this morning when I went in the shop and she was gone. I thought I was losing it. I mean there's no one around these parts who'd steal a neighbor's car."

"Unfortunately, there are a few. And I think that's a much more likely explanation than you losing it." Gramps was sharper than most people half his age. In fact, he was sharper than most people Colt could think of.

"You have an idea who it might be, then?"

Colt shrugged. "Not yet. I can think of a few who would, but until we look into it, I can't say I have any idea who did." He took the mug Gramps handed him.

"Come on out to the shop then. I don't know how you reckon you're going to figure anything out from looking out there, but I know you'll want to see."

Colt smiled as he followed him back outside. Another truck was pulling up beside his. Gramps's friend, Joe, got out and frowned at him. "You know who did it?"

"No, but I'll find out."

Joe grunted. "You'd better hope you figure it out before I do."

Gramps chuckled. "The kid will track 'em down and get her back." He grasped Colt's shoulder.

Joe scowled. "Maybe. But that ain't going to stop us from looking."

Gramps winked at Colt. "I don't reckon it will. There's fresh coffee in the pot. Why don't you go get one and catch up with us out there?"

Joe went into the house, and Colt and Gramps carried on toward the shop. "Did they take anything else?"

"Nope. And that tells me they're not too bright. If they had a couple of brain cells to rub together, they could have loaded her up with a couple of grand's worth of tools that were lying around within reach."

Colt didn't like to say that that made him wonder if whoever it was might be brighter than he'd suspected. An opportunist thief might have swiped everything valuable that they could quickly lay their hands on. But sometimes classic cars like Gramps's were stolen to order—and the ones that were were hardly ever recovered.

"Has anyone been up here recently?"

Gramps shook his head. "Jack and Em and little Isabel. Gabe was up here over the weekend talking about town business." He shook his head again. "Joe's here most days." He took a sip of his coffee and stared off at the mountains. "Shit."

"What?"

"Jimmy Hansen."

"When? Why?" Colt couldn't see any reason that the likes of him should come around Gramps's place.

"Damn, and I'm an old fool." Gramps looked pissed.

"Tell me."

"Last week. He stopped by asking if he could borrow a jack. Said he was working on getting a beater on the road for his girlfriend. I didn't think nothing of it. I mean, I know what he's like, but he talked a good story. Said he was trying to turn things around. Found himself a girlfriend and the girlfriend has a kid and he was trying …" He blew out a sigh. "Damn, and I'm an old fool."

"You're no fool, Gramps. There's no saying it was Jimmy and even …"

The look Gramps gave him stopped him short. "Don't treat me like one then. We both know there's an eighty or better percent chance it was him."

Colt nodded reluctantly. "Probably."

"Then don't stand around here, humoring me. Get on it. Look around the shop and see if there's anything that can help you here, then get your ass back to town, why don't you?"

Colt nodded. He planned to do just that.

"Do you want to have lunch today?"

Cassie smiled at Abbie. "Sure. I'd love to if we can make our timings work."

"We can unless you run late with Mrs. Abbott. Michael has no appointments between eleven and two because he's going over to the hospital. You're free between twelve and one thirty and I can take my lunch to match you."

"Great. Then, yes. I'd love to. And even if I run late, we can order something and eat here."

"Perfect," said Abbie. "Should we just do that? I can call Giuseppe's now and get them to deliver around twelve fifteen."

"Sounds good to me."

Abbie looked up and smiled when Ann Hemming came in.

"I'll email you my order," said Cassie before darting for her office. She liked Ann, but she'd told her story enough times this week already. It seemed every single patient who came in had wanted to know about her and Colt getting back together. It was nice that they cared, but it wasn't the best use of her time.

She sat down at her desk and fired up her computer. She had a lot of paperwork to catch up on before her first patient came in. She scanned the diary. It was going to be a busy day, and lunch with Abbie would be nice to break it up. Tomorrow looked set to be even busier. She smiled as she looked ahead. Friday was a little less hectic, and then there was the weekend. She didn't mind working Saturday mornings; she knew it helped people who worked all week and didn't want to take time off. Plus, it would make the time go faster until Colt finished his day.

The morning went by in a flurry. One patient followed another, and before she knew it, it was ten after twelve, and she was saying goodbye to Mrs. Abbott. She typed her notes on the visit before going out into the reception area. Abbie was paying the delivery driver for their lunch.

They took it through to the break room in the back, and Cassie took her wallet out of her purse. "How much do I owe you?"

Abbie waved a hand. "You can get it next time."

"Okay. Thanks."

Abbie grinned at her. "No problem. I'm glad you didn't argue with me."

Cassie knew better than to do that. As the doctor and the receptionist, she was fully aware of the difference in their salaries. But Abbie had made her pride very clear in the past. She paid her way and didn't take kindly to anything she saw as charity.

"But you can tell me how you and Colt are doing. I want to hear all about it."

Cassie smiled. "It's great, Abbs. It really is. In a way, it's like we've never been apart, but in other ways, it's even better. There's all the shared past that we have, but there's also this new guy—the man version, if you like."

Abbie chuckled. "And I have to say, you've got yourself quite a man. There are a lot of disappointed single women around here this week."

"I know. If he weren't Colt ... I mean ... if we weren't us... If we didn't have all the history that we do, I'm not sure I'd be comfortable. I'm not sure I would have dared go out with him."

"What do you mean?"

"I mean, I'm not the kind of girl you'd expect to end up with the sexy deputy sheriff. I'd expect a guy like him to be with someone more ... I don't know. You know what I mean."

Abbie frowned. "I think I do, but I don't like it. Yes, he's a good-looking guy, and he's popular with the ladies—or he would be if he'd give any of them a second glance. But you're quite a catch yourself, you know? Don't forget that."

Cassie shrugged. "I suppose."

"Suppose? You're a doctor, you're beautiful, successful, and all the things a guy would want. He's lucky to have you."

"Thanks. I suppose so."

"And where do you guys go from here—or haven't you talked about that yet? Sorry, I guess I'm just excited for you."

"No, it's okay. We haven't really talked about it. Well, not in any detail. We've made it clear that we both want what we always wanted—to end up together." She smiled. "Colt always knew he wanted to stay here and get married and have kids."

Abbie raised an eyebrow. "And that's what you want, too?"

Cassie nodded.

"Even the kids part?"

"Yes. I always said I wanted to have kids someday, but my career came first."

"Came first, or comes first?"

Cassie frowned. "I don't know. I haven't really thought about it yet. And we certainly haven't talked about it. We've only been back together a few days."

"Of course. Sorry, I'm being way too nosey."

"That's okay. You're making me think about it, and I need to. I've already told him that I want all the same things he does, so I should think about how that might look."

"Yeah."

Cassie thought about it as she picked at her salad. "I'm not getting any younger. If we're going to have kids …"

Abbie watched her.

She let out a self-conscious little laugh. "I do love kids, but I'm not so great with babies."

Abbie laughed. "I'm with you. I'm sure I'll be fine, but I do better with them when they're a bit older."

Cassie laughed with her. "Me too. It'd be nice if they came ready-made aged about six or seven."

"That'd be ideal."

"What are you two cackling about?" Michael had come in through the back door.

"Excuse me? Cackling?" Cassie asked indignantly. "You make us sound like a pair of witches."

Michael winked at her. "I said no such thing. I just wanted to join the fun."

"It was just girl talk."

"Oh. Okay."

Cassie smiled at Abbie and realized that they had become real friends. She didn't mind sharing personal stuff with her.

Michael grinned at them. "I know where I'm not wanted. I'll leave you two to your girly talk."

Cassie felt bad. "You don't need to do that."

"I know, but I figure if I pop back into town and bring cupcakes for dessert, you two can finish your chat, I'll earn some brownie points, and everyone will win."

"I do love win-wins," Cassie said with a smile.

"Great. I'll be back in a little while."

Chapter Eight

"How are you doing on Gramps's car?"

Colt made a face at Don. "I plan to take a drive over to the development at Four Mile Creek first thing in the morning."

Don frowned. "Why's that?"

"I haven't managed to catch up with Jimmy yet. I stopped by Kayleen's place, and he wasn't there, but apparently, he's been working on the construction site."

"Really? I would have thought Logan had more sense than to hire Jimmy."

"I thought so, too. I left Logan a message, but I haven't heard anything back yet. So, I plan on stopping by first thing. That way, I can talk to them both."

"I'll be interested to hear what you learn. And speaking of Kayleen, how did things seem at her place?"

"What do you mean?"

"Did you see little Sophie?"

"No. Kayleen said she was sleeping."

"Hmm. I heard she hadn't been in school."

Colt blew out a sigh. "I worry about her."

"You're not the only one. Mary took a shine to her when she went into the school to read to the kids. She's always talking about her."

"Maybe I'll stop back by the house again tomorrow and check up on her."

"Yeah, you do that." Don glanced at the clock. "Why don't you call it a day? I'm sure you have somewhere else you'd rather be."

Colt smiled. "You know it."

"Do I need to update your records to show the north shore as your home address?"

"No."

"Not yet?" Don asked with a grin.

"I don't know."

"Ah. You want her to move to town with you?"

Colt shrugged. "I don't think it matters, but ..."

"But you haven't even talked about it yet, and that matters?"

"Yes, that's exactly it."

"So, talk to her about it."

"I will."

As he drove home, Colt had to wonder why he hadn't talked to Cassie about it yet. He kind of knew the answer—he didn't want to rush things. He wanted to simply enjoy being together. He wanted to trust that everything would work out as it should, without needing to make a big deal out of anything. But at the same time, he wanted to know where they were heading.

He hadn't called her before he left work because he knew that she was probably on her way home, too. He smiled when he saw the garage door open and her car already there. He parked beside and it and hurried in through the back door.

"Hey, honey. I'm home," he called as he entered the kitchen.

She turned with a smile and came to wrap her arms around his neck. "Well, hello, Deputy Stevens. I've been waiting for you."

He lowered his head to kiss her and pulled her closer so he could feel her warm, soft body pressed against his. He loved the way she kissed him back, her kisses felt like coming home, in more ways than one.

He smiled when he finally lifted his head. "Hello, Dr. Stevens. I missed you."

He hoped he knew what she was thinking by the way she smiled. Their shared last name was how they'd first become friends. Cassie had been new to town in ninth grade. The class had sat alphabetically, and so she'd ended up right beside him, proving his friend, Austin's, claim that he was naturally lucky.

They'd been seventeen when Colt had first mentioned that her marrying him wouldn't be too much of a stretch since she wouldn't even have to change her name. Was she thinking about that now? It didn't feel like the right moment to ask.

"I missed you, too. I can't wait for the weekend to roll around so we can have a full day together."

"Me neither. But I love that we get to spend our evenings together."

"And our nights." Her hands closed around his ass and pulled him against her.

He closed his eyes and breathed her in. "I'm not going to be able to wait until nighttime if you keep that up."

To his disappointment, she let go of him and stepped away to stir a pot on the stove. "Sorry. I got a bit carried away."

He stood behind her and slid his arms around her waist, nibbling her neck as she stirred. "I can carry you away if you like."

She rested her head back against his shoulder. "I would like. But if we don't eat now, I won't want to." She planted a kiss on his cheek. "We can wait."

"Okay. Can I do anything to help?"

"No, it's almost ready. How was your day?"

"Not bad. How about you?"

"Business as usual. Coughs, colds, lady issues. I think flu season is starting to hit the school."

"Hmm. Have many of the kids been in to see you?"

"A few, yes."

"Was Sophie Wilson one of them?"

"No. Why?"

"Nothing."

She came to him. "There must be a reason you asked. What's wrong?"

"Probably nothing. I was at their place today. She's a sweet kid. Usually, she likes to chat to me, but her mom said she was sleeping. I thought that was odd; thought maybe she was sick."

Cassie looked thoughtful.

"Now, it's my turn to ask; what's wrong?"

"Probably nothing, but I worry about Sophie."

"Why?"

Cassie made a face. "It feels wrong to talk about it, but I guess since you'd be involved if there were an issue …"

"Tell me?"

"Sophie was one of the first patients I saw when I came back here. Her mom brought her in with tonsillitis. The poor little thing was wiped out, but …"

"But?"

"She had some bruises on her arms. She had a perfectly reasonable explanation for them, but I had a bad feeling. I talked to Kelly Miles … you must know her. She works for child and family services."

"I know Kelly well, unfortunately."

"She told me that they've been involved with the family for a while. The father isn't around and doesn't contribute, and the mother has a new boyfriend who …"

Colt sighed. "Who I'm currently investigating."

"Because of Sophie?"

"No. Unrelated. But if I had my way, he wouldn't be allowed within a hundred yards of Sophie."

"But there's nothing you can do?"

Colt shook his head sadly. "No. It's like Kelly always says—you can't police what might happen. I just hope I can get him on what has already happened. But even then, I doubt it'd be enough to put him away."

Cassie went to fetch plates from the cabinet. "It makes me so sad that some kids grow up in lives like that."

Colt nodded. He was no idealist. He knew that so many kids had it tough, but there was something about Sophie. She was such a bright little thing, and he hated knowing that her life would no doubt extinguish her spark before too long.

"Here." Cassie handed him a plate. "I'll let you serve yourself. I don't know how hungry you are."

"Thanks."

Cassie brought her plate and sat beside him at the table. "I swear to you, I'll do everything I can to make sure our kids have a wonderful childhood."

His heart buzzed in his chest, and he smiled at her. "You don't know how happy it makes me to hear you say that."

She chuckled. "What, you were worried I might be a mean mother?"

He laughed. "No. I mean to hear you talk about our kids like it's a given that we'll have them."

"I'd like it to be. If you still want to."

"I do. And we're not getting any younger." He wanted to kick himself as soon as he'd said it. He didn't want to rush her. Didn't want to pressure her.

He needn't have worried. She smiled. "I know. I don't want to be an older parent. I keep thinking it should feel weird talking like this when we've only been back together for such a short time, but it doesn't."

He took hold of her hand and squeezed it. "It feels right. It's what I always wanted. I think I have to let you take the lead, though."

She raised an eyebrow at him.

"I never had any doubts. You're the one who needs to be sure first that you're ready now."

"I am. I've known for a few years that I want a family. I'd like us to have some time to ourselves first." Her smiled faded. "We lost so many years."

"I'd like that, too. I don't mean I want to start a family right now."

"No, but sooner rather than later. And I don't see any reason why we shouldn't practice as much as possible."

"Practice?"

She waggled her eyebrows. "Making babies."

"Ah. Yep. I'm up for that."

She touched the front of his pants, making him close his eyes and suck in a deep breath.

"You are, aren't you?"

He hadn't been when he said it, but the feel of her fingers caressing him made his words come true. "Yes, and if you want to finish your dinner, you'd better stop that."

She gave him a wicked smile and took her hand back. "Sorry. Later."

He nodded, not sure how much later it'd be. He'd lost interest in dinner.

~ ~ ~

Cassie was tired when she got home on Friday night. It hadn't been a particularly hard week at work, but she was getting much less sleep than she was used to—not that she was complaining. As Colt had reminded her when he'd woken her this morning, they had a lot of time to make up for.

She was wondering if she shouldn't suggest that they spend this evening doing a little more, making up for lost time. They were supposed to be going to the Boathouse to meet up with the gang, but she'd much rather stay home—just the two of them.

She smiled when she heard Colt's truck pull into the garage, glad he was home on time. She'd wondered if he might be late. Home? She caught herself. This wasn't his home. She hoped it would be—and sooner rather than later, but they hadn't talked about any of that yet. She knew she was being a little selfish, too. He might prefer her to move in with him. His house was in town, much more convenient for him—and for her, if she were honest. But she didn't want to live there. It was just one of many things they'd have to figure out.

The door from the garage opened, and he greeted her with a smile and held out a bunch of roses.

"Oh! Thank you! They're lovely."

He dropped a kiss on her lips. "Not as lovely as you."

"Aww. Aren't you a smooth talker?"

He shrugged. "No. It occurred to me today that I'm really not. I haven't done anything to romance you at all. As soon as I knew that there was a chance for us, I took you back to my place, humped your brains out, and since then, we've fallen into a routine of sleeping together and going to work in the morning before coming home, and you cooking me dinner before we sleep together again."

He closed his arms around her. "I love you, Cassie. We have so much past, and it makes me happy that we're talking about our future, but that doesn't mean I should forget about the present. I want to make you happy every day, in little ways as well as big ones. So, I brought you flowers, and I want to take you out tonight and have a good time with our friends and dance and maybe walk on the beach when we come home—and then make love to you."

A rush of warmth filled her chest. He was right. They'd kind of fallen into a routine very quickly. She might be tired, but she loved the idea of a night out with him. They needed a date more than they needed to stay home like an old married couple.

She put her arms around his neck and looked up into his eyes. "I love you. Let's get ready and go out and have some fun."

His hands closed around her ass, and he held her against him. "Do you want to have some fun and then go out?"

Her pulse quickened as he rocked his hips against her. "Ooh. Yes."

He claimed her mouth in a deep kiss that left her breathless. When he lifted his head, he took her hand and led her upstairs. She moved toward the bed, but he tugged her hand and took her into the bathroom with a smile.

"I know you like to be efficient, so how about we take a shower and have some fun at the same time?"

She nodded eagerly and ran her tongue over her bottom lip as she watched him undress. He raised an eyebrow at her. "Are you coming?"

She chuckled. "Not yet, but I'm sure I will."

He smiled and helped her out of her dress. "I plan to make sure of it," he said as unhooked her bra.

He turned the water on and then held the door open for her. After he closed the door behind him, he backed her against the wall and claimed her mouth in another one of those deep kisses. His hands roved over her, making her moan as he slipped one between her legs and stroked.

She reached for him, but he moved his hips to the side. "You first."

She closed her eyes as he tormented her with his fingers, then lowered his head and teased her nipple with his tongue. She let her head fall back against the wall. He was driving her crazy. The feel of the warm water running over her body, his lips and tongue on her breasts and his fingers … Oh! Deep inside her thrusting over and over again, driving her toward the edge. She cupped his face between her hands and brought him back up to kiss her. He claimed her mouth, and that was all it took. She felt herself tighten around his fingers and moaned into his mouth as her orgasm took her. He didn't let up, thrusting deeper and harder as she shuddered and dug her fingers into his shoulders.

She let her head fall against his shoulder, breathing hard. "Colt," she breathed.

"I love you, Cass."

She nodded. "I love you, too—ooh!" She gasped at the feel of his hot, hard shaft pressing between her legs. "I need a minute."

He nibbled her neck. "You only think you do. Trust me?"

She nodded. She wasn't sure she believed him that she didn't need a minute, but she trusted him absolutely.

"Colt!" She gasped as he thrust his hips and filled her, sending aftershocks racing through her body.

He slid his hand down her thigh and lifted it to wrap around his waist. She gasped as he thrust deeper, and the aftershocks claimed her body in a full-blown orgasm. He showed her no mercy as he trapped her body against the wall and pounded deeper and deeper. She felt as though she were flying away. She was in that place—the place where reality ceased to exist and there was only the two of them. She claimed his mouth in a kiss and felt him tense. She needed him to join her. She raked her nails down his back and he did. He threw his head back as he found his release. "Cassie!" he gasped.

"Yes, yes, yes!" She moaned as she went with him again, clinging to him as they carried each other away.

Her legs were trembling as he let her foot slide back down to the floor. Water was running over his face as he smiled at her. "You're amazing," he breathed.

She touched his cheek. "You are. I love you so much."

He wrapped his arms around her and held her close to his chest. "I love you more. I don't want to spend another day without you, Cass."

She looked up into his eyes. "You don't ever have to. I'm all yours."

Chapter Nine

When they got to the Boathouse, Colt slung his arm around her shoulders as they made their way across the parking lot.

She turned and smiled up at him. "What's up? Do you need me to support you after your exertions?"

He laughed. "No. I'll admit my knees are still a bit wobbly, but this …" He tightened his arm around her shoulders. "This is me staking my claim. I want to hold you close to me, and I want the whole world to see and to know that you're with me, that we're together."

"Aww." She smiled. "To be fair, I think the whole world, or at least the whole town already knows that we're together."

"Yeah." He chuckled. "Gossip sure does travel fast around here." He held the door open for her and let her go in ahead of him. He frowned as he helped her out of her coat.

"What's wrong?"

"Noth …" he started to say but changed his mind. It was automatic for him not to talk about anything to do with work when he was out with his friends. But this was different. She was so much more than just a friend, and besides, she already knew why what he'd just seen would bother him. "Don't turn and look yet, because I just freaked him out by staring at him, but Jimmy Hansen is over there with Kayleen. They both look a bit worse for wear already."

Cassie made a face. "I wonder who's watching Sophie. Do you think she sees her dad on the weekends?"

"No." Colt would love to believe that Randy had stepped up and taken Sophie to his place, but he highly doubted it. The kid was probably with one of Kayleen's friends, and he thought no more highly of them than he did of her. "Come on." He took her coat. "We're here to have fun, not to get involved with that mess."

"Hey!" Kenzie greeted them with a grin when they got to the bar. "What can I get you guys? I feel like it should be champagne."

Cassie raised an eyebrow at her. "Are you running some kind of promotion?"

Kenzie laughed. "No! I mean to celebrate the two of you."

Colt grinned. "I think that's a great idea. What do you say, Cass?"

She nodded happily. "Why not. It's been far too long since I had any reason to drink bubbly."

For a moment, Colt wondered how long it had been and what the reason might have been—what had she felt like celebrating in the time they'd been apart. He caught himself. It didn't matter. It couldn't matter. As he'd already told her, there was no point in looking in the rearview mirror as they moved forward.

He looked around. It was still quiet for a Friday night, but he could see a few of their friends sitting at a big table over by the stage. Austin raised a hand, and he waved back. He should catch up with him. Austin was probably his closest friend, but they'd hardly seen each other in weeks.

Kenzie came back and set an ice bucket on the bar and handed him two flutes.

"Thanks, Kenz. What do I owe you?"

She laughed. "A wedding invite in due time. The champagne's on me."

"Thank you!"

She smiled. "You are most welcome. I just like to see everyone end up happy. I was worried that you two were going to take forever, but now I can check you off my list."

Cassie laughed. "And who's next on this list?"

Kenzie looked over at the table where Maria and Zack had just joined Logan and Roxy and Austin. "I think it has to be Austin, don't you?"

Colt made a face. "I don't know. I think he's enjoying his freedom since he and Olivia broke up."

Kenzie's lip curled. "Pft! Good riddance is about the nicest thing I can say about that one. What about Amber, though? I keep thinking that she and Austin are interested in each other, but …"

Colt wondered how much he should say. "What?" he asked innocently when he realized that both Cassie and Kenzie were staring at him, waiting for him to fill in the blanks. He held his hands up. "It's not my place to say."

"I'm only asking for an opinion, not insider information." Kenzie smiled innocently.

Cassie nodded. "I'm curious what you think, too."

He pursed his lips. "I think it's fairly obvious that he likes her. I don't know her that well. You'd probably have a better idea than I do about how she feels."

"You'd think so, wouldn't you?" asked Kenzie. "But I can't figure her out. She's friendly enough. She seems really sweet, but I don't know. I can't get anything out of her."

"Maybe she's just a private person?" suggested Cassie.

"You mean like you?" Kenzie smiled at her. "I have to tell you, I could not figure you out for the life of me."

Cassie shrugged. "Yeah. I'm sorry about that. I was acting like an idiot."

"Hey!" Colt put his arm around her shoulders. "You weren't—"

She laughed and shook her head. "I was, and we all know it. I just didn't know how to cope with being around you."

"Well, you do now." He dropped a kiss on her lips, surprised that she would be so open.

"I love it," said Kenzie. "Listen, I need to get back to work." She looked down the bar at a couple who'd just sat down. "But hopefully, I'll catch up with you later. And I need your orders for the Valentine's dinner."

Colt frowned. "What Valentine's dinner?"

Kenzie laughed as she walked away. "Ask the others about it. I've only been mentioning it to the couples since I know Valentine's can be a bummer when you're on your own."

He turned back to Cassie. "Do you want to have our own little bubbly celebration before we join everyone?"

She looked at the bottle, then at him, then at the table where all their friends were now sitting. "No. Let's go and share it with them, shall we?"

He grinned, happy that she wanted to include their friends. "I'd love to."

~ ~ ~

When they reached the table, Maria eyed the champagne and then looked up at Cassie and Colt.

"Is it safe to assume that the two of you have figured things out?"

Colt looked at Cassie, and she smiled. "Yes. It is." She leaned against him, and he put his arm around her shoulders. "We're drinking bubbly to celebrate the fact that we're putting years of misunderstandings behind us—and the fact that I can stop behaving so badly whenever he's around now."

They all laughed at that.

"I could never figure that out," said Austin. "It just wasn't like you."

Cassie smiled at him. "I know, and I'm sorry I was such a pain in the butt."

"You weren't a pain in the butt. It was weird, that's all. I'm just happy you've worked it out." He nodded at Colt. The two of them had always been close, and Cassie could only imagine what they'd shared over the years that she'd been gone.

Logan grinned at her. "I'll be the one to say it. You were a pain in the butt. But if you crack open the bubbly and I get some before it's all gone, then I'll forgive you."

Cassie laughed. "I knew I could rely on you, Perkins."

Roxy shrugged beside him. "I'd apologize, but you already know what he's like."

"I do."

"We all do." Colt opened the champagne and then looked around when he realized he only had two flutes. "Do you want to go get some more glasses from Kenzie, Logan?"

"I think the two of you should drink it," said Roxy. "Enjoy it. It sounds like it's been a long time coming."

Cassie took the glass Colt handed to her and raised it to chink against his. He held her gaze for a moment before he murmured, "Forever takes a while."

She felt tears prick behind her eyes, and she nodded. "It does, but I think we're on the home stretch now."

She could see the love shining in his eyes as he took a sip of his champagne. "I'd say we are."

Everyone scooted along when Angel and Luke arrived to join them. There still weren't enough seats for everyone, though. Colt caught Cassie's eye and patted his thigh. She smiled as she happily gave up her chair and sat on his lap.

Logan grinned at them. "That's what I like to see."

Abbie caught Cassie's eye and made a face before she spoke. "We don't all need to hear your opinion every time, Logan. I've been telling you that since we were ten."

Roxy laughed. "Thank you. I've tried telling him that, too, but he doesn't listen to me."

Abbie smiled at her. "If I thought I was treading on your toes, I'd keep quiet, but I know you need all the help you can get—and possibly a medal for putting up with him."

"Aww." Roxy put her arm around Logan's shoulders. "No. He's a sweetheart, really."

Logan batted his eyelashes and smiled. "See. I'm misunderstood, that's all. But Roxy gets me."

Cassie had to laugh. She would never have expected to see Logan behave the way he did with Roxy. All through high school, and as far as she knew, ever since, he'd been a ... a player was a nice way of saying it, she supposed.

Jade, who had just arrived with her sister, Amber, looked around at them all. "Will someone help me get this straight once and for all? Who all grew up here, and who didn't?"

Cassie looked around, expecting someone to explain, but they all looked at her. "Okay. I guess I will. Let's see. I believe that Colt, Austin, Logan, and Abbie all grew up here. I came at the end of middle school, and then ..." She looked around, making sure she wasn't missing anyone. "Luke and Zack came to the flight school and met Angel and Maria, who both came here for jobs ... is that right?"

Angel smiled at her. "It is. I came to work at the lodge at Four Mile when it opened."

"And I came with Laura to work at her jewelry store at the plaza," added Maria.

"Thanks," said Jade. "I get confused with everyone. Some folks never left, some are newcomers, and some moved away and came back."

"That's right," said Austin. "And you two fall into that last group, right?"

Jade shrugged. "I suppose so, but we moved away when we were so small that it doesn't really count. I don't remember ever coming here till Lenny had her heart attack."

"No," added Amber. "I always wanted to come and see this place, but ..." Jade shot her a look that made Cassie wonder what she'd been about to say.

"And don't forget Ivan," Austin spoke up in the awkward silence that followed.

"Shoot. I'm sorry, Ivan." Cassie smiled at him. "I'm not sure I'd know how to say where you came from."

Abbie's fiancée smiled at her. She didn't know him that well, but he seemed like a good guy, and she knew that both Abbie and Colt thought the world of him. "I work for Seymour Davenport. I came with him when he moved here to be with Chris."

Jade smiled at him. "Yeah. We've been here longer than you have, I know you."

"Uh-oh." Everyone looked at Logan and then followed his gaze. Cassie's heart sank when she saw Jimmy and Kayleen standing near the bar arguing. She looked at Colt, and he gave her an apologetic smile and started to get to his feet.

"Hold on a minute, bud." Logan smiled at him. "Kenzie's on her way."

Cassie had to smile. She knew Kenzie was a formidable force, and she could probably de-escalate the situation. Still, she got up from Colt's lap and squeezed his hand as he watched. He wouldn't step in if he wasn't needed, but he was ready in case he was.

~ ~ ~

Colt frowned as Jimmy started to wave his hands around and grow more agitated. This looked like it was about to get out of control. He started to move toward them but stopped after a couple of steps when Kenzie reached them. He should give her the chance to deal with it first.

He smiled as she stepped between them and said something to Jimmy. His expression hardened, and he said something back. Kenzie stepped toward him and got right up in his face. Colt started toward them but again stopped and had to smile. He couldn't imagine what Kenzie had said but instead of yelling at her—or worse—Jimmy nodded and said something with a smile. Kenzie smiled back before turning to Kayleen. Kayleen didn't look as amused, but she nodded.

Colt shook his head in wonder as Kenzie led them to two empty stools at the end of the bar. They exchanged a few words that looked like things might be taking another turn for the worst, but Kenzie went back behind the bar and mixed two cocktails in a shaker before pouring them with a smile and encouraging them to drink up.

Colt wasn't sure that giving them more alcohol was the best way to go, but at least it had them smiling and not fighting. He blew out a sigh and looked at Cassie. She looked as relieved as he felt.

Logan grinned at him. "Didn't I tell you? Kenzie's something else."

"She is," Colt agreed. He knew she'd diffused many situations in here, but he hadn't seen her in action before.

"She's got more balls than I have, too," said Logan. "No way would I get up in Jimmy's face like that."

"No one in their right mind would. Well, no one other than Kenzie." Colt frowned. "You never called me back about him."

Logan cocked his head to one side. "Jimmy?"

"Yeah. I didn't catch you on site yesterday morning, and I left you a voicemail."

"Shoot. You did. Sorry."

Colt realized the others were all watching them. "Mind if I steal your man for a minute, Rox?"

"Be my guest."

Logan followed him to the back of the restaurant. "What's up? What makes you think I know anything about Jimmy?"

"I imagine you know more than most people do if he's working for you. I hope you have some reason to trust him."

Logan laughed. "Do you realize how crazy you sound? Why in the hell would I hire Jimmy Hansen? And why would anyone ever trust him?"

Colt frowned. "Kayleen said he was working at Four Mile."

"Not for me, he isn't. You know what it took me to build a team of good guys over there. No way would I poison the well by bringing Jimmy in. He's as crooked as they come."

"Have you seen him over that way at all?" Colt's mind was racing. Why would Kayleen lie to him? Maybe she didn't know it was a lie? Maybe she was only repeating what Jimmy had told her?

Logan nodded. "Yeah, now you mention it. I did see him the other morning out on East Shore. I remember thinking that it was weird to see him out that early in the morning."

"Where did you see him?"

"Like I said, on East Shore Road, he was turned off on the forest service road. That's why it caught my attention. I thought whoever was driving, pulling an enclosed trailer, must be crazy to try and take it up there in the winter. I laughed when I saw it was Jimmy because I knew I was right. He is one crazy dude."

"What was the trailer like?"

"Plain, white." Logan shrugged. "Maybe twenty-five feet long. Like a car hauler type thing."

Colt nodded and glanced over at Jimmy. He and Kayleen seemed to have forgotten their argument and were all over each other. It made him wonder what Kenzie might have put in their drinks.

"Why all the questions, anyway?"

"I can't say."

Logan made a face. "Maybe if you said more, then I'd know what was important and return your calls sooner and let you know when I see weird stuff, instead of laughing it off."

"You're right. Sorry. Gramps's Chevelle was stolen last week."

"Shit!" Logan glanced over at Jimmy. "See! If I'd known about that, I would have stopped to see what Jimmy had in that trailer."

"Yeah, and probably gotten yourself into a fight or worse."

"Maybe, but I would have called you. Damn. I'll bet he's got the Chevelle up there somewhere."

"Either that or he's already passed it on."

"Do you want to go up there and see if we can find it?"

Colt pursed his lips and thought about it.

Logan grinned. "Come on. For all you know he might be keeping it hidden up there till someone comes to get it tomorrow. And don't worry about Cassie, she'll understand."

Colt glanced over at her. He knew she would, but he didn't want her to have to. He'd told her that he wanted to bring her out on a real date, to dance together, to walk on the beach afterward. Going off to see if he could find Gramps's car didn't exactly fit with his idea of giving her a great evening.

She caught him looking at her and smiled. He knew she'd understand. And he also knew that this might be the perfect opportunity to recover the car. The thought of how happy that would make Gramps swayed him. "I'll go and have a word with her, but I need to check in with the office. I'll get Anthony to go up there with me."

Logan made a face. "You need me to show you where it is."

Colt laughed. "You don't know where it is. You don't even know if it's up there. You told me you saw Jimmy turning onto the road. You can only guess where he went."

"Yeah, but I want to come."

Colt blew out a sigh. "Come on. Let's talk to Cassie first, then I'll talk to Don."

Cassie raised an eyebrow at him when he got back to the table. "Is everything okay?"

"Yes, but Logan might have figured out where Gramps's car is."

"That's great!" She gave him a rueful smile. "But you're looking wary because you think you should go and try to get it back right now?"

He nodded reluctantly. "It wouldn't surprise me if it's been hidden until it can be picked up."

"And for all we know, it might be getting picked up tomorrow, so it's now or never, right?"

He nodded again. "I'm sorry, Cass."

She smiled. "Don't be. It's your job. And ..." She glanced over at Jimmy and Kayleen. "If it's him, then I'd rather you went now while we know where he is and can be sure that he won't show up and surprise you."

"True. I feel bad leaving you here, though."

She planted a kiss on his lips. "There's no need. I'm used to coming out with everyone by myself."

"I know, but I want you to get used to being out with me."

"We have the rest of our lives to do that."

He hugged her to him. Grateful that she was so understanding. "I'm hoping I'll make it back before the end of the night."

"I'm fine. I can take a cab home. If I do, I'll let you know when I leave."

"And when you get home, too?"

"Okay. But you have to keep me posted, too—to let me know you're safe."

"I will."

Chapter Ten

Cassie yawned as she walked across the parking lot to the back door of the medical center. She hadn't gotten much sleep last night—but not for the usual reason. Colt hadn't come home until three a.m.

She and Roxy had stayed out with everyone else until almost one. They'd both hoped that Colt and Logan might come back while there was still some evening left to enjoy. But Colt had texted her when he could and kept her abreast of things as they searched the area around the trailhead. She'd been thrilled when they'd found the trailer with Gramps's car inside. Everyone had, but it'd been strange sitting there just a few yards away from Jimmy knowing what was going on when he had no idea.

She smiled at the smell of coffee when she let herself into the break room. Abbie greeted her with a smile. "Morning. I figured we'd both need plenty of caffeine to get through this morning. It's only been a few hours since we said goodnight."

"Thanks. I need it." She took the mug Abbie handed her with a grateful smile.

"Was it really late when Colt got home?"

"About three."

"Wow. So, you've barely had any sleep. And what's the story? Can they pin it on Jimmy?"

"It sounds like it. Colt's back at work this morning."

"Will they go and arrest Jimmy?"

"I really don't know how it all works. I think they have to have enough evidence first." Cassie guessed that there might be more to it than that, too. If Jimmy had been hiding the car for someone else to collect, then she imagined that Colt would want to see if he couldn't catch them, too.

Abbie smiled. "If you're going to be the sheriff's wife, you might want to get a better handle on how things work."

Cassie laughed. "He's not the sheriff; he's a deputy."

"For now, maybe. But I bet he will be when Don retires." Abbie gave her a knowing smile. "And it's telling that that's the detail you picked up on."

"What do you mean?"

"You corrected me that he's not the sheriff. You didn't correct me that you're not his wife yet."

Cassie smiled. "I didn't, did I?"

"Nope."

"Anyway. What does the morning look like?"

"Business as usual, mostly. A couple of regular checkups, a couple of probable flu cases, and …" Abbie shook her head. "That's all I can remember. I told you. I need caffeine to wake my brain up."

For once, the morning seemed to go by slowly. Usually, Saturday mornings went by in a blur, and she was finished before she knew that she'd started. Maybe it was because she was tired or maybe because she was looking forward to seeing Colt tonight, but the time dragged.

She washed her hands at the end of her mid-morning break and stuck her head into Abbie's office. "Everything okay out here?"

"Yeah." Abbie glanced out at the waiting room and then slid down from her chair with a frown. "We have a couple of walk-ins. I was hoping to catch you." She came to the door and stepped out into the hallway where Cassie was standing, closing the door behind her so that the patients in the waiting room wouldn't hear.

"What's wrong?"

"I hope nothing, but I have a weird feeling. I've had a couple of people call asking if anyone could see them if they came in. I said yes to the first three—I always save three slots on a Saturday. The fourth one I should have told no. But I couldn't make myself do it."

"Why? Who was it?"

"Kayleen Wilson."

Cassie's heart started to race. "What's wrong with her?"

"It's not her. It's little Sophie. Apparently, she fell in the yard when she was playing. Hurt her arm."

Cassie scowled. "But you don't think it was play and you don't think she did it herself?"

Abbie held her hands up. "If I only go by the conversation—by the words spoken, I should have no reason to question it. But, Cassie, I have a bad feeling."

"I do, too. When are they coming?"

"I told her to bring her straight in."

"Good. Is anyone out there in bad shape?"

"No. No one's urgent."

"Okay then, when Kayleen gets here, let me know, and I'll see them next."

"Thanks, Cass. Hopefully, I'm being silly."

"We can hope so. But if you are, then I am, too. I have the same feeling. Send Mrs. Carter in now. Maybe Kayleen will arrive by the time I'm done with her."

It took another half an hour before Abbie buzzed to say that Kayleen had arrived. Cassie was just getting finished with Marianne Benson, who was still suffering from migraines.

Marianne smiled at her. "Thanks, Cassie. I'm sorry to take up your time with my headaches."

"Don't ever apologize. We're going to get them under control. Will you ask Abbie to make you an appointment in two weeks, and we'll see how you're doing?"

Marianne made a face. "How about I just call for an appointment if I'm not doing any better?"

"No. I know you. You don't want to be a bother, and I'm telling you, you're not a bother. I want you to come in and keep coming in until we find a combination that's going to help."

"Okay. Thanks. I will. See you in a couple weeks then."

"Bye."

Cassie quickly made some notes before she buzzed Abbie. "Ask Kayleen to come through."

"Right."

A moment later, her office door opened, and Abbie stood there looking agitated. "I wanted a word with you first. I think we were both right. I think you're going to need to call Kelly Miles."

Cassie's heart sank. "Is Sophie okay?"

Abbie made a face. "You're the one who's qualified to say that, but my guess is no. Kayleen either, but I'm not so worried about her, she's making her own decisions, bad as they may be. Poor little Sophie gets no choice in the matter."

"Okay. Send them in." Cassie took a deep breath to steel herself. She wasn't looking forward to this, but she was prepared to do whatever was needed.

The door opened a few moments later, and little Sophie came in, followed by her mother. Sophie was cradling her right arm in her left. She looked subdued, to say the least. Kayleen moved as though she was a much older woman.

Cassie forced herself to smile at them. "Hi, Sophie. What did you do to your arm?"

The little girl frowned. "I didn't—"

"She fell when she was climbing the fence." Kayleen spoke over her and shot Sophie a warning look. "I think she might have sprained it."

Cassie pressed her lips together, then smiled at Sophie again. "Do you mind if I take a look? Do you want to get up on there for me?" She nodded toward the bed by the wall.

Sophie nodded and went over to it. As she climbed on—
nimbly to say she was only using one arm—her T-shirt rode
up, and Cassie winced when she saw bruises on her back.

"I just need to step outside for a moment." She smiled at
Sophie. "I'll be right back." Kayleen eyed her warily.

Cassie's shoulders sank as she stepped out into the hallway.
She had no real proof yet, but she wanted backup. She tapped
on the office door, and Abbie came out. "Do me a favor and
call Kelly? See if she can come over here. I don't know for
certain that we need her yet—and you can tell her that—but
I'd like her here."

"Will do. Are you going to look at Kayleen, too?"

Cassie raised an eyebrow.

"By the looks of her, I'd say Jimmy went after both of
them."

Cassie swallowed. "Okay."

When she went back into her office, Sophie smiled, and
Kayleen narrowed her eyes. "What's going on?"

Cassie forced a smile. "I just needed a word with Abbie."
She turned to Sophie. "Let's have a look at that arm, shall we?"

Sophie nodded and held it up. "Mommy says it's sprained,
but I think it's broken."

After a brief examination, Cassie was inclined to agree with
her. She'd have to get her to the hospital for x-rays. "Did you
hurt anything else?"

Sophie shrugged and glanced at her mother.

Kayleen scowled at Cassie. "We're here about her arm. Do
you think it's broken?"

Cassie nodded slowly. "I do. I'd like to get her to the hospital for x-rays and …" She held Kayleen's gaze. "I'd like to check her over, see if she hurt anything else."

Kayleen got to her feet quickly and winced. "There's no need for that."

"I think there is." Cassie looked at Sophie. "Do you mind if I look at your back?"

Sophie nodded eagerly and lifted her T-shirt as best she could with one arm. Cassie's blood boiled as she saw the bruising. "How did that happen?"

Kayleen came and pulled the T-shirt back down. "I told you. She fell climbing the fence."

Cassie turned to her. "Did you fall off the fence too?"

Kayleen's jaw worked, but she didn't reply.

"Want to tell me what really happened?"

Kayleen shook her head and tears shone in her eyes. "I told you already. Come on, Sophie. We're leaving."

Cassie was glad that the little girl didn't move an inch. She glared at her mother. "I don't want to."

Kayleen moved toward her, but Cassie put herself between them. "Please let me finish?"

For a moment, she thought Kayleen was going to push her out of the way and grab Sophie. Instead, she collapsed back onto the chair. "It's her fault. Jimmy told her to be quiet this morning."

Cassie's heart raced. "What happened?"

"She made too much noise. Woke him up. And he took it out on us."

Cassie nodded. "Do you want to press charges?"

Kayleen looked at her as though she'd lost her mind. "Hell, no! I want to get Sophie's arm fixed and go home. He'll be mad if we're out all day."

Cassie couldn't believe what she was hearing. "You seriously want to take your daughter back into the house with him there?"

Kayleen scowled. "I told you. It was her fault. Not Jimmy's."

Cassie looked at Sophie.

"I don't want to go back there."

"You shut up."

A surge of relief washed over Cassie when the buzzer sounded. "Kelly's here," announced Abbie.

"Send her in."

Kayleen got to her feet again. "You bitch! You called Kelly Miles?"

Cassie nodded. "My priority here is Sophie. I would have thought that she was yours, too."

Kayleen glared at her, and Cassie let out a deep breath when the door opened, and Kelly came in.

"Kayleen. Sophie."

"Hi, Ms. Miles." Sophie seemed pleased to her, but Kayleen was livid.

"What do you want?"

"Same as always. To make sure Sophie's okay."

"It's always about Sophie. What about me?"

"What about you?" Kelly raised an eyebrow at her. "Are you ready to send Jimmy packing?"

"No!"

"Then I can't help you. I've told you before, Kayleen. Your first step has to be to get Jimmy out of your house and out of your lives."

"That's not happening."

Kelly looked at Cassie. "Are you done here?"

Cassie shook her head. "Sophie's going to need to go to the hospital. Her arm's most likely fractured."

Kelly nodded. "Want to ride with me, Sophie?"

Sophie smiled. "Yes, please."

Kayleen glared at them. "And what am I supposed to do?"

"Come with us, if you'd like." Cassie was impressed by Kelly's matter-of-fact attitude.

"What about Jimmy?"

"You know my answer to that."

"I need to get home. He'll be mad."

"That's your choice. But Sophie needs to go to the hospital. Are you coming with us or not?"

It blew Cassie's mind when Kayleen shook her head slowly. "No. I can come and pick her up later … or can you drop her home?"

Kelly's voice remained calm and even, but Cassie got the impression that she didn't feel as calm as she looked. "We'll have to see about that. She might not be able to come home until Jimmy's gone."

"He's not going anywhere."

Kelly nodded curtly. "Then we'll talk later. Come on, Sophie."

Cassie was amazed at the way the little girl smiled when she slid down from the bed. "Bye, Dr. Stevens."

"Bye, Sophie."

She didn't even look at her mother as she followed Kelly out.

When they'd gone, Cassie looked at Kayleen. There were so many questions she wanted to ask her. She stuck with the only one that pertained to her job. "Are you okay … are you hurt?"

Kayleen stared at her for a long moment. "I'll be fine."

Cassie stared back at her. She didn't know what to say.

"You don't understand."

"You're right. I don't. She's your daughter."

Kayleen shrugged. "Yeah, but Jimmy …"

Cassie shook her head sadly. "She's your daughter."

"You don't have kids, do you?"

"Not yet, no."

"You'll see. It's not easy. They mess up your life."

Wow! Cassie shook her head. "I'm sorry you feel that way."

Kayleen nodded. "I never wanted her."

Cassie had to bite back her anger. "Is there anyone else she could go with? Her father? Relatives?"

Kayleen let out a bitter laugh. "Randy's useless. My family's mostly gone—dead or in prison."

"I see." Cassie knew she really didn't see. She couldn't imagine what that kind of life would be like. All she knew was that she wished Sophie could break free of it.

"I'd better go."

Cassie nodded. "There are people who'd help, you know. Help you and Sophie. I will if you'll let me."

Kayleen stopped at the door and looked back at her. "There's no helping me. If it worries you that much, why don't you help Sophie yourself? Do us both a favor?"

She walked out, and Cassie stared for a long time at the space in the doorway where she'd been standing.

~ ~ ~

Colt rubbed his eyes as he made his way downstairs on Sunday morning. The sun was streaming in through the living room windows already. He'd slept late. So much for them having a fun Saturday night and lazy Sunday morning together. He'd worked until almost midnight last night, and judging by how high the sun was in the sky, it was almost midday now.

He found Cassie sitting on the window seat that looked out over the lake reading a book.

"Good morning, beautiful. I'm sorry."

She smiled and got to her feet. "I've told you before, there's no need to be sorry. It comes with the job; I know that. I'm sure there'll be times when I'm the one who has to work late and sleep late. I get it. Are you hungry?"

He shook his head. "Not yet. I appreciate the offer, but I need to wake up first."

"Coffee?"

He grinned. "Always."

They settled on the sofa, and he sipped his coffee, feeling it slowly bring him back to life. "How did your day go yesterday?"

She made a face. "I thought you might have heard."

"Heard what?"

"About Sophie?"

He shook his head. "I was crazy busy all day. The good news is that I think we're going to be able to bring Jimmy in."

"That is good news." Cassie shuddered.

"What?"

She told him about her visit with Sophie yesterday—and about her leaving with Kelly. "Kayleen didn't even seem to care." She shook her head sadly. "I still can't quite believe it, even though I was there. I can't believe a mother could care more about her boyfriend than her child—that she'd let Sophie go with Kelly. Surely, she understands that she might not get her back?"

"Yeah. I think she knows that. I'm surprised I didn't hear from Kelly."

Cassie shrugged. "I called her this morning, but only got her voicemail. It makes me so sad for Sophie."

Colt rubbed her arm. "Don't be sad."

"I can't help it. She deserves so much better."

"I know she does, but ..." He sighed. "I feel the same way, but I can't afford to let it get to me. There are hundreds, thousands of Sophies out there. It's sad, but it's true. It's just how life is. We can only do what we can. And we both do the jobs we do because we want to do as much as we can."

"Exactly. I want to do something for Sophie."

Colt shook his head. "It's not our place. She's in good hands with Kelly. But even she has to work within the system. The goal is always to keep the family together where possible."

"I know!" He was surprised at the frustration in her voice. "But sometimes that shouldn't be the goal. Sometimes the family doesn't even want to be kept together. Sophie didn't even look at her mother when she left. Kayleen was more worried about Jimmy—who obviously hits them—than she was about Sophie."

"Maybe we'll be able to put Jimmy away. Then he'll be out of the picture."

Cassie met his gaze. She was so beautiful. "I almost hope he doesn't go to prison. If he stays in the home, Kelly won't let Sophie go back there. And if she's forced to choose, Kayleen will choose Jimmy every time."

Colt thought about it, but he knew it wasn't their place to figure it out—much as he'd love to. He dealt with the care system often enough to know that mostly the status quo was maintained. Cassie was new to it all. It horrified her, and he wished it still did him. But he'd been hardened to it over the years. Yes, he'd love to see Sophie placed in a home full of love, but that wasn't likely to happen. What was likely was that she'd end up moving from foster home to foster home or in a group home setting. And when faced with that, life with her mom might not be so terrible—if he could get Jimmy out of there.

Chapter Eleven

"How many years has it been since we did this?"

Colt slung his arm around her shoulders as they walked. "Too many."

She looked up at him and smiled. "Good answer."

"It's the right answer. In fact, I think we should make a pact right now."

"What kind of pact?"

"That we'll never let another year go by without coming down here to walk on this beach."

"Aww. I like that idea. Though, if we move, if I sell the house, we'd be trespassing if we walked down here."

He hugged her closer into his side. "True. But I don't think you ever want to sell this place, do you?"

"No. But I will if that's what's best for us."

He stopped walking and slid his arms around her waist. "Is it bugging you, too?"

She raised an eyebrow, but he thought she knew what he meant.

"We haven't talked about where we want to live—where we want to build our life."

"Yeah. It has been on my mind. I know I'm being selfish. I always ask you to come here."

"You know I'll never say no."

"Exactly. I do. But I know you love your house, too. You're just as attached to it as I am to this place."

Colt looked up at the house. It was beautiful, especially in the late afternoon sun. "No. I do love my house, but not as much as you love this place. It is more practical, though."

She chuckled. "Of course, it is, and if you're trying to appeal to my practical side, that should, in theory, work. But it doesn't for some reason. I know it's a drive from here into town, and that might be an issue over the years—for us going to work and …"

She seemed hesitant to say it, so he finished the sentence for her. "And for our kids going to school."

She smiled. "Yep. But then, I did it."

Colt stopped walking as a thought struck him. "I hope we have all boys."

"Why?" Cassie's eyes were wide.

He laughed. "Because if we have a daughter, one day she'll want to date. And I can't deal with the idea of some kid driving her home up here like I used to drive you."

She laughed. "At least we'll know every spot they might stop to make out on the way home."

Colt shuddered, and he was only half faking it. "She may never be allowed to date."

"You'll get used to it. I mean, if she dates a guy like you, then I'll consider her—and us—very lucky."

"She could do worse," he agreed as they walked on. "So, are we reaching the conclusion that we want to live here?"

"I believe we are. I feel as though I should squash what I want and agree to whatever you want, but …"

"No! I don't want you to ever do that, Cass. We both have to be honest about what we want and figure out how to make us both happy."

"I know. But when it's an either-or situation like this, then one of us has to compromise."

"And I'm prepared to. I'm more concerned that we get to live together than where we do it." He smiled. "And now that we've figured out the where, I can ask you officially: Do you want to live together?"

"Yes! I do. Do you want to move in with me?"

"I feel like I kind of already have, but yeah. And I want to bring some of my stuff, too."

She chuckled. "You want to bring your clutter up here?"

He narrowed his eyes at her. "It's not clutter."

She laughed. "I know. I'm only teasing."

Colt stopped abruptly when he saw movement farther up the beach.

"What is it?"

He squinted, trying to make it out, then he relaxed. "Sorry. I think it's Pete and Holly. See? Up by the rocks?"

She shaded her eyes as she peered to where he pointed. "Oh, yeah."

Pete had spotted them, too, and waved.

"Do you want to go over there?" she asked.

"Sure. I haven't seen Pete yet to thank him for interfering."

She laughed. "Oh, I'm sure he's so pleased with himself that he won't mind waiting to be thanked."

When they'd almost reached them, Colt saw little Noah sitting playing with pebbles. That explained why Pete was squatting down like that.

"Hey, guys!" Holly greeted them with a grin. "Great minds think alike, huh? It's such a beautiful day, and finally a bit warmer. We had to come down here."

Pete grinned at Colt, and Colt nodded at him. "When we saw you, we had to come over. I haven't had a chance to thank you."

Holly waved a hand at him. "Please don't. He's full of himself as it is."

Cassie laughed at the way Pete pouted. "I'm proud of myself—proud of helping my friends out, not full of myself."

Holly went to him and patted his shoulder. "Yes, Pete. Whatever you say, Pete. You did well, okay?"

He nodded and laughed. "Seriously. I'm happy for you." He looked at Colt. "So, can we expect to see more of you up here now—on a permanent basis?"

Holly frowned at him. "Don't put them on the spot like that."

"It's okay." Colt smiled at her and put his arm around Cassie's shoulders. "The answer is yes. I'm going to be up here full time from now on."

Pete grinned. "That's great news."

"It is," Holly agreed. "And it means we should have you over for dinner, welcome you to the neighborhood."

Cassie looked at him. "Oops. I was supposed to ask if you wanted to come over for dinner with everyone this week."

Pete scooped Noah up, and the little guy laughed. "Don't worry about that. You probably don't want to be subjected to kiddie night, but we can set something up soon, maybe ask Jack and Em, too. They're your other neighbors after all."

"What's kiddie night?" asked Colt.

Cassie laughed. "See, I told you he might like that idea."

Pete raised an eyebrow at him. "It's when all the couples with kids come over. It's easier than trying to bring the kids out for dinner, and we don't have to subject the others—who don't have any—to the little people.

Colt smiled at him, and he looked puzzled for a moment until realization dawned.

"Oh! I remember. You love kids, don't you?"

Colt nodded happily and waved at Noah, who waved back at him and burbled something that only he understood.

Pete came closer and held him out toward Colt. "You want to?"

Colt took him happily. "Hey, little buddy. How are you doing?"

Noah waved his pudgy little fist and burbled again. It sounded as though he had a lot to say about something.

Holly laughed. "You seriously are the kiddie whisperer."

Colt laughed. "I don't know about that. But I do love them."

~ ~ ~

Cassie's heart clenched in her chest as she watched Colt with Noah. Could she really be so lucky? If she had to describe him, she'd say he was a man's man much more than a ladies' man. He was big and tough, and he knew how to take care of himself and the people he cared about. She'd always known he loved kids, but seeing him with Noah turned her to mush. He was so strong and so gentle all at the same time. And they'd just talked about it; one day, in the not-too-distant future, he'd hold their child that way.

Holly caught her eye and nodded. She understood.

Pete raised his eyebrows at her. "I hope I'm not putting my foot in it here?"

She laughed. "Not at all. It's wonderful."

"It is?" He looked wary.

"It really is. When I used to talk about career coming first, I meant chronologically—not in my order of priorities. I always wanted to have a family someday, but I needed to get my career on track first." She smiled at Colt. "And now it's firmly on track."

Pete nodded. "Are you saying that we might get to invite you to kiddie night as participants rather than just observers?"

She nodded happily. "I hope so."

It was dark by the time they got back to the house. "Do you want a drink?" she asked as she went around turning the lights on.

"I brought wine," said Colt. "If you'd like some? I thought we could sit out with blankets and watch the moon come up."

Her eyes filled with tears. He was still so thoughtful. She went to him and slid her arms up around his neck. "How did I get so lucky?"

"I'm the lucky one."

She frowned. "I don't think that's true. You do all kinds of things for me. I …" It struck her that she didn't do thoughtful little things for him.

"Hey." He tucked his fingers under her chin and made her look up into his eyes. "You do all kinds of things for me. You always have."

She didn't think that was true, but she resolved to make sure that she would do more in the future.

She brought the blankets out while he poured the wine. It was cold and crisp. There were no clouds after a sunny day, and the stars shone brightly. She snuggled against him under the blanket and looked up at the clear sky.

"It's so beautiful."

"Make the most of the stars while you can."

She smiled. "I know. They'll be dimmer when the moon comes up and starts to shine."

He laughed. They'd had so many conversations about that when they were kids. Intelligent as she was, he just couldn't get it through to her that the moon didn't shine—it only reflected the light of the sun. "You won't be able to see them as well after the moon rises ... how about that?"

She winked at him. "Okay. We'll leave it at that. How long do we have?"

He checked his watch. "It should be coming any minute now." He pointed to the horizon in the east. "I think it should appear over there. But it might take a little bit longer to rise up over the mountains."

She smiled as she watched him talk. "I don't mind waiting."

He looked down into her eyes. She couldn't resist. She cupped his face between her hands and pulled him down into a kiss. She loved the way he kissed her; she always had, but there was something different about this kiss—something special. His arms closed around her, and she slid her fingers into his hair as their mouths told each other so much more than words could ever express. She knew she'd look back on that kiss as the official start of their new life together.

When they finally came up for air, he hugged her closer to his chest. "I love you, Cass."

"I love you, too. Oh, look!" She pointed to what looked like a star hovering just above the mountains. As they watched, it grew bigger and gradually showed itself as the moon—a bright, full, perfect moon that slowly rose into the dark sky and bathed the night in a beautiful silver sheen.

~ ~ ~

Colt smiled to himself as he turned off West Shore Road into Gramps's driveway. Times like this were part of what made him love his job.

He parked in front of the house and smiled when Gramps and his friend Joe came out onto the porch.

Gramps grinned at him. "You're a good un, kid."

Colt smiled back at him. "Just doing my job."

"I don't think it's in your job description to use your own truck to return stolen property."

Colt looked at his truck. It'd made sense to use it to tow the trailer up here. He shrugged. "It's no big deal. I wanted you to have the car back as soon as possible."

Joe nodded. "You moved fast. I thought it'd be while a before you got it back up here, and here you are before Monday's even over."

Colt went to open the back of the trailer and let the ramp down. "Do you want to unload her here?"

"Sure thing." Gramps looked wary. "Is she any worse for wear?"

"Nope. There's not a scratch on her."

"That's a relief."

"Yeah. From what we can figure out, Jimmy had a buyer lined up to come and collect it yesterday."

Gramps scowled. "And what's going to happen to him?"

"He'll probably get off with a slap on his wrist and a warning not to do it again," said Joe.

Colt straightened up. "You know I don't decide what happens to him. If I did, I think you'd be happier with my form of justice. But I only get to bring them in. And in this case …" He shook his head.

The two older men looked at him. "What?" asked Gramps. "Don't tell me you can't nail it on him?"

Joe pursed his lips. "He's skipped town?" asked Joe.

Colt nodded reluctantly. "Don's had the guys looking for him since Saturday."

"And Kayleen doesn't know where he is?" asked Gramps.

Colt made a face. "There's no sign of her either."

"Did the little girl show up for school this morning?" asked Joe.

"She did. But she wasn't with her mother." Colt hesitated but didn't see any harm in telling them. The way the rumor mill worked, they'd hear soon enough anyway. "Kelly Miles took her to the hospital on Saturday."

Gramps shook his head sadly. "Some people shouldn't be allowed to have kids."

Joe nodded beside him. "Sounds like Kelly decided that Kayleen's one of 'em. But the kid's okay? She can't be too bad if she's at school this morning."

"Yeah. Her arm's broken, but she's okay."

"That's good." Gramps looked relieved. "Anyway, let's get the car back in the shop. Sounds like maybe it all turned out for the best."

Colt raised an eyebrow.

"If having my car go missing for a few days was what it took to get that little girl out of that situation, then it was worth it. Hell, I'd have given Jimmy the car to drive away in if'n I'd known it'd get him away from her."

Colt nodded. He'd always loved Gramps and hearing him say that just made him love him more. "Do you want me to back her out of the trailer for you?"

Gramps grinned. "I'm good. I'm not such an old fart that I can't squeeze in there and get her out."

Colt stood next to Joe to watch as he backed the Chevelle out of the trailer and then revved it a few times and kicked up some gravel as he gunned it toward the shop.

Joe grinned as he watched. "You didn't seriously think he'd let you drive it, did you? He's never let me drive that one, and I've been asking for forty years."

Colt laughed. "Hey, I had to try. Don wouldn't let me take her for a spin when I loaded her up either. Told me I had to ask Gramps ... now I know the answer."

Gramps stuck his head out of the shop door. "You coming in?"

"I wish I could, but my day's not over yet."

Joe grasped his shoulder. "Well, when it is over, you can go home tonight knowing that you did good today."

"Thanks."

Gramps came out and shook his hand. "Thanks, Colt. You give my best to Cassie, you hear me? And one of these days you bring her over for a visit. Be nice to see her someplace other than the medical center."

"Thanks, Gramps. I will."

By the time he'd returned the trailer to the yard and filled out the paperwork, it was time for him to knock off for the day.

He stuck his head in Don's office on the way out. "I'll see you tomorrow, boss."

Don looked up and took his glasses off. "Okay. I'm going to need you to pay a call on Randy tomorrow."

Colt's heart sank. "What's he done now?"

"It's not what he's done. It's what we need him to do."

"What's that?"

"Well, with Kayleen and Jimmy gone, Kelly's going to want to talk to him."

Colt blew out a sigh. "You know he's not going to step up."

"Sure, I do. But he's little Sophie's father. CPS's priority is to keep the child with family, where possible."

"But in this case, it's definitely not desirable, and probably not possible."

"I'm with you. But you know we have to go by the book. So, tomorrow, you'll be having a chat with Randy, maybe bringing him in to have a chat with Kelly."

Colt sighed again. "Okay. I'll talk to her first before I go over to Randy's. Where's Sophie staying in the meantime?"

"Kelly found her a short-term placement with one of her families. But it can only be short term. You need to see what you can do with Randy."

"You really think it's in Sophie's best interests for me to convince Randy to take her?"

Don shook his head. "You tell me, Colt. What do you want me to do? If it were up to Mary, I'd bring the kid home to live with us, but that's not realistic. Out of the options available, Randy might not be so bad."

Colt stared at him for a long moment. He knew he was right, but it broke his heart that he couldn't find some way to help little Sophie find a better life.

Chapter Twelve

"Is it me, or has this been the longest week ever?" asked Abbie.

"It's not just you," said Michael. "I feel the same way. I think it's this time of year. It's cold. The days are short and dark. Christmas is a fading memory, and there's nothing on the horizon to look forward to any time soon."

Cassie laughed. "It must have been a long week to have you talking like that. You're normally so upbeat."

Michael grinned. "I'm not on a downer or anything. It's just this isn't my favorite time of year. I'm looking forward to blue skies and warmer weather. And they're not coming any time soon, and there's nothing fun going on either."

"I know what you mean," said Abbie. "But, there is something coming up—Valentine's dinner."

Michael shrugged. "I know, but I don't think we're going to make it. My folks are out of town that weekend." He grinned. "I think he's taking her away for a romantic weekend, but he won't admit it, just says they haven't had a break for a while."

"Aww, that's so sweet," said Abbie. "I love your folks, they're awesome."

"They are," agreed Cassie. "And if you're short of someone to babysit, I don't mind doing it."

Michael laughed. "You've got to be kidding me, darl'? The first Valentine's day that you and Colt are back together and you're going to spend it watching Billy and Ethan so we can go out? I don't think so."

"Yeah," agreed Abbie. "You can't do it." She gave Michael an apologetic smile. "And I can't either."

"That's okay. I know. Everyone has their own plans. And besides, Megan and I can have a good time at home."

"What about one of the singles?" asked Cassie.

"Really, it's not a problem. We're going to stay home and have a nice dinner." Michael waggled his eyebrows. "I intend to make sure she's not disappointed."

"Michael!" Abbie slapped his arm.

"What?" he asked innocently. "I don't want my lady to be disappointed about not going out, and you think that's a problem?"

Abbie laughed. "You can't wiggle out of it. We know what you meant, and we don't need to hear about it, thank you."

Michael shrugged. "Whatever." He glanced at the clock up on the wall. "I suppose we'd better get this day rolling. At least it's Friday."

"Yep, and I'm not in tomorrow," Abbie said with a smile.

Michael nodded. "You enjoy your Saturday off while we slave away in here."

Abbie laughed. "I'll take you both out for lunch today if you like. You know, so I won't feel guilty tomorrow."

"Nah. I'm only messing with you, darl'. You do a great job for us. You've really knocked this place into shape. You deserve your time off. And I'd love to come to lunch, but I want to run over to the library and surprise Meggie today. Take her for a bite."

Cassie loved the way he was always thinking about his wife and their two boys.

Abbie looked at her. "Are you going to blow me off as well? Do you have plans with Colt for lunch?"

"No. No plans. He rarely gets time for lunch."

"Well, his loss is my gain."

Michael nodded. "We should close up and all get out of here. It'll do us good."

Cassie nodded. "Okay. Where do you want to go, Abbie?"

Abbie laughed. "Well, we have such a wide range of choices. We could go to the Boathouse, the bakery, or Giuseppe's."

"I've got dibs on Giuseppe's," said Michael.

"How about the bakery for a change then?" Cassie looked at Abbie.

"Fine by me."

They all looked up when the buzzer sounded, announcing that the first patient had arrived.

Cassie got to her feet. "That's probably Mrs. Carter. I'll get to my office."

Abbie followed her out. "Have fun," she said with a smile. "Only four and a half hours to go."

The morning went by quickly, and soon they were walking into the bakery for lunch.

"Mm." Abbie sniffed the air as they went in. "I love the smell in here."

April smiled at them from behind the counter. "Hey, ladies. What can I get you?"

"A table, please," said Cassie. "We're here for lunch."

"Great. Seat yourselves wherever you like. I'll be right over."

They took a table by the window, and April came over with menus and took their orders. When she'd gone, Cassie looked out the window. Main Street was quiet, but then it seemed that everything was quiet at this time of year. She smiled when she saw Austin hurrying down the sidewalk.

Abbie followed her gaze. "I like Austin. He's good people."

"He is. Honestly, I feel bad about him."

Abbie frowned. "Why's that?"

"He and Colt are good friends, and since Colt and I figured things out, we've spent all our time together. I don't think he and Austin have seen each other at all."

"That's the way it goes, though, isn't it? Especially in the beginning. You'll find your groove soon and figure out how to work in time for yourselves and your friends."

"I suppose so. Is that how it's worked out for you and Ivan?"

Abbie's smile lit up her face. She always looked like that when they talked about Ivan. "Kind of, but neither of us really had close friends before we got together. I was …" She shrugged. "I hadn't really gotten my act together since I came back here, and Ivan was pretty new in town. Actually, I think he hung out with Colt and Austin if he hung out at all. Maybe we should plan to do some girly stuff so that they can have their guy time."

Cassie smiled. "I'd like that."

"Yeah, me too." Abbie nodded happily.

"Hi, ladies." Austin waved at them as he came in.

"Hey, Austin. How are you?"

He shrugged. "Keeping busy." He came over to their table. "At least, I'm trying to keep busy. This time of year is always slow. It's kind of dull and dreary, and I guess I'm feeling kind of that way myself."

"We were just talking about that this morning," said Cassie.

Austin smiled at her. "Yeah, but I'm sure it doesn't make any difference to you. I mean, the sun's finally shining in your world."

She smiled back happily. "It really is. I'm sorry, though. I've kind of been hogging him, haven't I?"

Austin laughed. "There's no need to apologize. I'm happy for you both. It's been such a long time coming, and if I'm honest, I wasn't sure that you'd ever get back together."

"For a few years there, neither was I. But seriously, Austin. I don't want to be the girlfriend who elbows her way in and means that you two don't get your guy time anymore."

He waved a hand at her. "Don't worry about it. It'll all work out. Colt and I have been friends since we were born. We don't need to be in each other's pockets. You come first now, and that's as it should be."

Abbie smiled at him. "We need to find you someone, too."

Austin's smile faded. "I'm good, thanks."

"What, you mean you wouldn't like to have someone of your own to spend time with—someone who comes first for you?"

He pursed his lips. "Honestly? I spent the last couple of years dating someone who demanded that I put her first." He blew out a sigh. "I'm enjoying getting to call my own shots these days."

Cassie smiled at him. "I think that's good. You need to be able to be your own priority, get straight with yourself before you can make room for someone else."

He smiled back at her. "Exactly. Even if I were to meet someone now, I don't think it would work. Not yet."

Cassie nodded. She knew that he'd dated Olivia for a couple of years. And having gone to school with her, Cassie could understand why he'd need time to recover from that.

April came back with their sandwiches and set them down. "Enjoy, ladies. I have your order ready whenever you are, Austin."

"Thanks. I'll be right there."

"Are you planning to eat at your desk?" asked Abbie. "You could join us."

"No, thanks. My order is sandwiches and pastries for a meeting I have this afternoon."

"Is business good?" asked Cassie.

"It's booming. Sales have stayed steady through the winter. Most of the vacation homes have long-term tenants." His expression changed.

"What's wrong?"

"Oh, nothing. Just talking about long-term tenants reminded me. I have one who's skipped town, and I'm waiting to see what I can do there."

"Kayleen and Jimmy?" asked Cassie.

He nodded. "Yeah. It should only have been her, but he's been living there since they got together."

"What'll happen now?" asked Abbie. "Can the landlord just assume that they've gone for good and take the place back?"

He made a face. "Well, fortunately, I guess—depending on how you look at it—I'm the landlord. I did Kayleen a favor renting the place to her—I only did it because of Sophie. So, at least, I'm the one on the hook ... not someone else. But there's a clause in the lease that if they abandon the property for more than fourteen days, I can take possession back again. I think it'll be that simple. I don't see them coming back any time soon."

Cassie nodded. "I think you're right about that, although what it'll mean for Sophie, I don't know."

Austin shook his head. "I heard that Kelly placed her with the Murrays, but I doubt she'll be able to stay there for very long."

"Why's that?" asked Abbie.

"They already have a full house. They've been fostering for years. One of the older kids is away for a couple of weeks visiting family in the city. They took Sophie as a favor to Kelly, but she won't be able to stay when the boy comes back."

"That's a shame," said Cassie. "I hope Kelly will be able to find a family for her."

"Me too." Austin checked his watch. "I should get going. It's nice to see you both."

"And you. Are you coming out this weekend?"

"I'd love to." Austin smiled. "I should get out while I can. I don't imagine I'll see anyone next weekend. You'll all be caught up in Valentine's stuff."

Abbie gave him a sly smile. "Not everyone's coupled up. You could hang out with Amber."

Cassie noticed a touch of color in his cheeks, but he shrugged it off. "It's not as though she's by herself. I imagine she'll be hanging out with Jade."

Abbie rolled her eyes. "Are you deliberately being dumb? I meant you could ask her out."

Cassie felt bad for him, wishing that Abbie had let it slide.

Austin shrugged. "I told you. I'm not ready to start dating again yet. I don't think I'd be any use to anyone."

Cassie smiled at him. "You take your time; you'll know when you're ready. And in the meantime, how would you feel about coming up to North Cove for dinner one night?"

"Sure, that'd be great." He didn't sound too convinced.

"I hope you will. It'd give you and Colt a chance to catch up—and me, too."

He smiled. "Okay. Give me a call and let me know when."

"I will."

Once he'd gone, Abbie smiled at her. "You guys were all in the same group of friends in high school, weren't you?"

"We were, and I meant what I said. Of course, I'd like for him and Colt to catch up, but even apart from that, I'd like to catch up with Austin, too."

"I didn't realize that Olivia had done such a number on him."

"Neither did I, but I can see it. I never did like her."

Abbie shuddered. "Me neither. I don't know what he saw in her."

Cassie laughed. "I'm not sure he ever had much of a choice in the matter. The way Colt tells it, once she set her sights on him, he just kind of went along with it. And before he knew it, a couple of years had gone by."

"That's so sad!"

"It is, but at least he's out of it now."

"Thank goodness. I just hope it doesn't take him too long to get over it. I think Amber likes him, too, but she's not going to wait around forever."

"I hope they get together. I think they'd make a great couple, but we'll just have to wait and see. Things tend to work out as they're supposed to."

Abbie nodded. "Yeah, but I think you'd be the first to admit that sometimes it takes a bit longer than you'd like."

"I know. I know."

~ ~ ~

Colt stopped by his house after work. He'd been taking a few of his things up to Cassie's place with him each night. He let himself in and looked around the living room with a smile. It wasn't cluttered. He just liked to collect things. There were pictures on every wall—either souvenirs from his travels or just colors and scenes that he liked. His bookshelves were overflowing; that wasn't clutter. No one would ever convince

him that books were clutter. To him, they were many things—
they were adventures to go on, new information and ideas to
explore and learn. He looked at the entertainment center.
Okay, so maybe he didn't need all the hundreds of DVDs
anymore; he didn't remember the last time he'd watched one.
He streamed his movies and TV these days, but ... he
shrugged. Okay, maybe they were clutter. He didn't need to
take them to Cassie's.

He did need his clothes, though. He ran upstairs and started
filling a duffel bag with jeans and workout gear—his work
uniforms had all been at Cassie's for weeks now. He pulled his
phone out and dialed her number.

"Hey, you," she answered. "Are you on the way or working
late?"

"I'm finished. I'm at my place getting some more stuff. I
wondered if you want me to pick something up for dinner."

"Hmm. I was thinking about making something, but I
couldn't decide what."

"So, how about you don't bother. I can call an order in to
the Boathouse now and pick it up on my way back out of
town."

"Okay, thanks. Would you get me the salmon?"

"Sure." He almost asked if she wanted anything for dessert
but thought better of it. If he asked, she'd say no because she
didn't think she should. But if he showed up with something,
she'd love it. "Do you need me to get anything else while I'm
in town?"

"No. I think we have everything we need. Just bring yourself
home to me. I miss you."

He smiled. "I miss you, too. I'll be as quick as I can."

Twenty minutes later, he stood at the take-out counter at the end of the bar. It was Friday night, but it was still early, and the place was quiet.

Kenzie spotted him and came over. "Don't tell me you're here drinking alone already? Where's Cassie?"

He laughed. "Nope. She's at home, waiting for me to pick up dinner."

"Oh!" Kenzie laughed with him. "I should have known. I almost made that mistake once before."

"What mistake?"

She laughed again. "When Michael and Megan first got together, I gave him a hard time for coming out without her, and he was only getting dinner to take home to her."

"I hope you didn't give him too hard a time?"

Kenzie made a face. "It's all in the past now."

"I'm glad I was able to set you straight right away. I saw you put Jimmy Hansen in his place last weekend. I'd hate to get on your bad side."

She gave him a rueful smile. "Yeah. In another lifetime, I had to be pretty tough. I got good at putting assholes in their place. You're not one of those, though; you're safe. But Jimmy …?" She pursed her lips. "I'm glad he's gone. And Kayleen, too. She's a piece of work, that one."

Colt nodded and blew out a sigh.

"What's up? Don't feel bad that you didn't pick him up before he left town. If you had, he'd probably still be walking around causing trouble. This way, he's banished himself. And good riddance is what I say."

"It's not that."

"What, then?"

"I was thinking about Sophie."

"Oh, I know. She's a little sweetie. But she's better off anyway." She frowned. "Though … is she? I hadn't really thought about it. I mean, she's better off away from her mom and Jimmy, but what happens to her?"

"Well, Kelly Miles is her case manager."

"Oh, I adore Kelly! She's awesome, and Marla, they both are. Sorry. What about Sophie?"

"Well, Kelly was hoping that she'd be able to place her with her father."

"Pft! Randy? He's no better … actually, no, I take that back. He's not mean. He's useless, but he's way better than Jimmy, if only because he's too lazy to be mean. But what's Kelly going to do now?"

"Now what?"

"You said she wanted to place Sophie with him, but he's gone, too."

"What!?"

"Oh, shit! You didn't know?"

"I went out to see him on Tuesday. And I only talked to him yesterday."

"From what I've heard, he was already gone yesterday."

"What have you heard?"

"That his dad was taken into the hospital, and he had to leave in a hurry to go see him."

Colt frowned. "When did you hear this?"

"Last night."

"That's impossible. I talked to him yesterday. He didn't mention anything about his dad or going to see his dad. It's impossible."

Kenzie made a face. "Either impossible or bullshit. Sounds like he wasn't too keen on the idea of being a real dad to Sophie, so he bailed—and made up a story to make it sound like he had reason to go."

"Jesus!"

"I know, right? Some people should be neutered so they can't produce offspring. Poor little Sophie's no better off than a stray kitten now."

He had to laugh. "I'd love to disagree with you, but Jimmy and Randy are both prime candidates."

"Yup. And if you can get a law passed to approve it, I'd volunteer to do the lopping."

Colt cringed at the thought of it. "I was thinking of something more humane, maybe chemical?"

Kenzie laughed. "Where's the fun in that?"

He laughed with her and turned when Lia came out of the kitchen with his order. "One salmon steak, one black and bleu burger, one cheesecake, and a death-by-chocolate."

"That's right." Colt handed his card over.

"Say hi to Cassie for me," said Kenzie. "And enjoy your dinner. Just hearing that made me hungry."

Lia looked up. "Do you want me to do you a burger before it gets busy?"

She grinned. "Yes, please."

Lia laughed. "And follow it up with a death-by-chocolate?"

"Not only yes, but hell, yeah."

Colt smiled and picked the bag up from the counter. "Have yourself a good night. I hope Chase gets to eat here, too."

"Of course he does. He's not even here yet, but we'll eat before he and Eddie set up for the night."

"Well, give him my best. I think we're coming in tomorrow night."

"Good, we'll see you then."

Chapter Thirteen

Cassie smiled when she heard Colt's truck pull into the garage. She was glad that he'd offered to pick up dinner for them. Not only because she loved the salmon steak but more so because it'd given her some time to do a couple things around the house rather than cooking.

Colt had been slowly moving his things here, but so far, he'd only hung a few of his clothes in the closet and put his socks and undies in one of the drawers she'd cleared for him in the dresser. Most of his clothes were still in bags, and he hadn't opened any of the boxes he'd brought, let alone found places to put his things. She wanted that to change.

She'd always teased him about his clutter—all their friends had. He was one of those people who had a lot of things. When they were kids, he'd had shelves full of DVDs and video games, and books, too. His bedroom walls had been covered with posters. And on the few occasions that she'd been to his house since they got back together, she'd seen that he hadn't changed. Granted, there were more books and paintings and carvings than he'd had before. But the overall impression was still the same—he kept a lot of clutter.

She, on the other hand, was more minimalist. She liked clean lines and clean, empty surfaces. But this was going to be their home—not just hers—and she wanted him to be able to live comfortably. She'd emptied the shelves in the living room—which had taken two minutes since each shelf only displayed one item. Her vase, candle, framed diploma, and the picture of a sunset didn't need all that space to themselves. Not when Colt could fit so many books and other knickknacks there.

She'd also cleared half the closet and several more drawers in the dresser. She'd only been using that space as storage—for clothes she rarely wore. She had a whole stacking system of boxes she could use for that in one of the spare rooms.

She went to him when he came in from the garage and slid her arms up around his neck. "Hi."

He set the take-out bag down on the counter and pulled her to him. "Hey." He dropped a kiss on her lips. "How was your day?"

"It was okay. I had lunch with Abbie, oh, and we ran into Austin. I invited him to come up here for dinner soon. I know you haven't had a chance to catch up with him, and when I suggested that the two of you should go out for a drink, he didn't want to take you away from me." She laughed. "So, I thought I'd invite him up here."

He held her closer and nodded happily. "Thanks. I appreciate that. It's been bugging me that I haven't made time to see him lately."

"I know, and it's my fault."

"Nope. It's my choice."

"Well, now you don't have to choose."

"Thanks, Cass."

"You're welcome. Everything's been going so well for us, but I don't want to get complacent."

"What do you mean?"

"I mean that we've gotten back together and moved in together and gotten back on track so quickly, and I love it. But I don't want little things to go unnoticed until they become problems. Things like you still having time for your friends." She took his hand and led him into the living room. "And having room to put your things." She gestured toward the now-empty shelving. "I made space for you." She tugged his hand and took him into the bedroom and then the closet. "You need more than a sock drawer. This is your home, too, now."

"Sometimes, I think you read my mind. Thanks, Cass. I brought some stuff back with me, but I didn't want to bring too much. I know you don't like my clutter."

She slid her arms up around his neck. "No. I don't like clutter in general. But when it comes to you, it's different. I love your clutter because it's a part of who you are—and I love you."

He chuckled and slid his arms around her waist, holding her to him. "I think claiming to love it might be going a little too far, but I know what you mean, and I appreciate it more than you know. It'll help me feel more at home here. More like we're living together than like I'm living at your place."

"Exactly, that's what I want. I want this to be our place, our home. We can joke about clutter and drawer space, but we have to be realistic—it's the little things like that that could become problems if we don't address them now. And Austin, too, and other friends. It's natural, I think that we want to spend all our time together in the beginning. But I don't want you to neglect your friendships. It wouldn't be right—or healthy."

"I know, and I don't want you to neglect yours—"

"I …" She stopped and smiled.

"What?"

"I agree with you. I was about to say that I don't have friends here, but it's not true. I do. Abbie and I have gotten close since I came back. And the other girls, too. I was kind of holding back before we got together, but now I want to reconnect with the girls and get to know the newcomers better."

He smiled. "Sounds like you're ready to start building your life here."

"I am. That's exactly what I want to do." She wanted to add that she felt like it was time to get married and settle down and start a family, but she didn't want to feel as though she was rushing him. She knew that was what he'd always wanted, but it felt wrong for her to have been gone all this time and then come back and demand it as soon as she was ready.

He led her back out to the kitchen. "Thanks, Cass. It means the world to me that you're doing what you can to show me that you really want it now."

She opened the bag and sniffed. "Oh, that smells so good."

"Yeah. We should eat before it gets too cold."

She turned to get plates from the cabinet but stopped and turned back around. As she'd suspected, Colt had already opened his box and started picking at fries. "Do you need a plate?"

He grinned. "I'll take one if you're handing them out, but I don't *need* one."

She laughed. "One more little compromise." She came back and set her own box next to his on the island.

"Don't let me stop you if you want to use a plate."

"Actually, I think I prefer it this way. I think it'll do me good to check my habits and see which ones mean anything to me, and which don't. I always use a plate for take-out, but there's no need. In fact, this is better; it means no dishes to do later, either." She stole one of his fries and popped it in her mouth with a smile.

He laughed. "I think we can both pick things up from each other. On some things, I'll come around to your way of thinking, too."

"Maybe."

"But I hope that when it comes to take-out, you'll be happy to come over to the dark side."

She laughed. "I'd hardly call this the dark side."

"What about death-by-chocolate?"

"Ooh! I could be persuaded on occasion." She looked at the bag and noted with disappointment that it was empty.

He chuckled. "Don't look so sad. I did get it. It's still in the truck. I was going to surprise you, but I can't finish my burger while you look so sad."

"Oops. You weren't even supposed to see that."

"I notice everything about you, Cass. I know what makes you happy. I know when you're disappointed—and I don't ever want to disappoint you, not even over chocolate cake."

"Aww." She rested her head against his shoulder. "Has anyone ever told you you're the best?"

"Yeah. You used to tell me that all the time."

"And now I'm telling you again, and I'll keep telling you because it's true. You are the best, Colt. The best man I've ever known and the best thing that ever happened to me." To her surprise, she teared up and had to swallow.

"Hey." He put his hand on her shoulder. "I thought that made you happy—not sad."

She shook her head and swallowed again, swiping at the tear that escaped and rolled down her cheek. "I'm sad for all the time we lost. All the years we'll never get back. We didn't need to be starting our lives now. We could have had it all by now."

He put his arm around her shoulders. "I have to believe that everything works out as it's supposed to, Cass. We don't know what might have happened if we'd stayed together as kids. You might have ended up resenting me if you didn't go away to school. I might have resented you if I'd gone with you. I know I've said it before, but you just can't go through life looking in the rearview mirror, wondering about what might have been. We can only go forward and get started on our forever now."

"You're right. As always. It's just that when we used to say that—that forever takes a while—I thought it meant that it would take just a couple of years. I don't think I would ever have left if I'd known that it'd be more than ten years until we got back together."

"And that's what I'm saying. If you hadn't left, we might have ended up breaking up for real, never getting a chance at forever. This way, it hasn't been easy, but, at least, we get our chance now, when we're old enough and wise enough to make the most of it."

"I know." She blew out a sigh. "I didn't mean to get all weepy on you. It just hit me."

He hugged her into his side. "It hits me sometimes, too, and I want to scream and throw things and demand that life give us back the years we lost, but ..." He shrugged. "None of that's realistic, is it? So, I make the most of what is—and I think about all those things I just told you; that maybe this is how things were always supposed to work out for us."

She looked into his eyes and planted a kiss on his lips. "Someone as good-looking as you are shouldn't be allowed to be so wise, too."

He laughed. "Okay, I'll shut up."

"No! I'm being serious."

"Yeah, right. You're the smart one."

"Maybe at book learning, but there's a difference between education and wisdom. And you, my love, are one very wise man."

He swaggered his shoulders. "Why, thank you. I'm not going to argue with you. But tell me more about the good-looking part."

She laughed. "As if you didn't know all about it."

"Nah."

"Don't give me that. Every girl in town calls you the hot deputy."

He batted his eyelashes. "I'm not interested in the girls in town. I want to hear what the sexy doctor thinks."

"You know what she thinks."

"Tell me."

"I think you're gorgeous."

He put his hand on her thigh. "Do you think I'm sexy?"

She nodded breathlessly—her food forgotten. "I think you're the sexiest man I've ever laid eyes on."

He ducked his head and nipped her bottom lip. "I always knew you were the most beautiful girl in the world; now you're the most beautiful woman. Are you finished here?"

She stared at him, not knowing what he meant.

"Your dinner."

"Oh. That." She shook her head. "Food is the last thing on my mind right now."

His smile sent shivers racing down her spine. "Want to tell me what the first thing is?" He got to his feet and took her hand.

"You."

"What about me?"

"The things you do to me."

He was walking her slowly toward the bedroom but stopped and looked down into her eyes. "What things?"

"The way you kiss me."

His arm snaked around her waist and crushed her to him as his mouth claimed hers in a kiss that left her breathless. "Like that?" he asked when they finally came up for air.

"Yes. Like that."

"What else do I do to you?"

She met his gaze and smiled. "You can do whatever you want to me."

"I want you to tell me."

She bit her bottom lip and pressed her thighs together. He was making her whole body hum with desire for him. "I love the way you feel when you hold me close."

His arms tightened around her waist. "Like this?"

She nodded and closed her eyes at the feel of his hard-on pressing against her. "I love the way you push my skirt up."

When he did, she sucked in a deep breath. The rough fabric of his uniform pants against her bare skin only heightened her need for him.

"What about when I take your panties down?"

She nodded with a whimper as he did. "Yes! That, too. And when you unfasten your pants, but don't even get out of them because ..."

She leaned back against the cabinets when he let go of her to unzip himself.

"And when you kiss me—"

The way he claimed her mouth told her that he'd heard all he needed to. His hands closed around her ass, and he lifted her onto the counter. She clung to his shoulders and gasped when he thrust his hips and filled her. They moved together frantically, their bodies melding into one. She let her head fall back as the pleasure built inside her, then moaned when he mouthed her breast through her blouse.

"Come for me, Cassie."

His words sent ripples of excitement racing through her. This was a new side of him, and she was loving it. He'd always been able to take her there whenever he wanted to, but telling her to? That was new. She liked it and ...

He thrust deeper and harder, driving her to the edge. "Come for me."

His words tipped her over, and she let herself go. "Yes!" she agreed as her orgasm took her. It was enough to take him, too. She felt him tense and find his release deep inside her. They clung to each other as they took each other back—back to the place where only they could go.

When they finally stilled, she kissed him deeply. "I love everything about you. Everything you are." She smiled. "And everything you do to me."

He cupped her face between his hands and looked deep into her eyes. "Ditto. And you know, this seems like the perfect time to remind you that a while doesn't have to take forever."

"What do you mean?"

He smiled. "We've been back together for a while now."

She nodded.

His smile faltered. "How long of a while do you need before we can get on with forever?"

She still didn't understand.

"Cass. We both keep saying that we want kids and we want a family. Are you ready for that yet? For kids and everything that goes with it?"

"I am."

"It's not too soon?"

She thought she knew what he meant. They hadn't been back together very long—was it too soon to get married? She shook her head. "I think we've already lost enough time, don't you?"

He smiled. "I do. It's like I said before, though, there are some things that once we talk about them, we can't take them back. I've been scared to say it, in case you need more time."

She cupped his face between her hands. "You told me a long time ago that it wouldn't be a big stretch for me to marry you since I won't even have to change my name. You were right, and I'm ready whenever you are. I didn't want to bring it up because I didn't want to march back into your life and demand that you marry me now—now that I'm ready, but it's what I want, Colt. Whenever you want to."

He hugged her to his chest but didn't speak. She could only hope that meant he was happy.

Chapter Fourteen

Colt smiled when his phone rang on the way home. They were going out tonight to meet up with the gang at the Boathouse. Cassie was probably calling him to see if he'd finished work yet—or if she should go on alone. He loved that she was so understanding about his job—and independent enough that she was happy to do her own thing if he got caught up.

He hit the button on the steering wheel to answer. "Hey."

He was surprised when a male voice filled the cab. He didn't immediately recognize who it was.

"Is this Colt?"

"Yes. Who's this?"

"It's Randy."

"Randy! Where the hell are you?"

"I'm in Oakland. My dad took ill, and I had to come help out."

Colt frowned. He didn't believe that story. "I see. And what can I do for you?"

"I wanted to ask you about Sophie."

"What about her? It's Kelly you need to talk to."

"I don't do well with her. I just want to know that Sophie's okay."

Colt shook his head.

"Are you still there?"

"Yeah. What do you want to know?"

"Like I said. I want to know that she's okay. I'm not cut out to be her dad, but I do care about her, you know. Did they find a place for her to stay?"

Colt didn't even want to reassure him of that. "Temporarily, yes. She's with a family in town, but she won't be able to stay there for long. Do you plan to come back and take her in yourself? Because if you don't, I don't know what will happen to her. She probably won't be able to stay in Summer Lake. She might get placed with a family in the city or put into a group home."

"She's a sweet little thing. Someone will take her in, don't you think?"

"Sweet as she is, if her own parents won't take her, what makes you think someone else will?"

Randy was quiet for a long moment. "Do you know anyone? There are lots of good people at the lake … people with money … people who could give her a much better life than I ever could. Or her mother."

"Are you still looking to get out of paying child support?" Colt tried to suppress his anger, but he knew it came through in his voice.

"Not just that. I want her to have a chance. I know you think I'm an asshole—and you're right. But you can't argue that she deserves a chance in life. I talked to some people here, and they said that if she's put into care, me and Kayleen will both have to pay, but if we give up our rights—if she gets adopted, or something—then we wouldn't be responsible for her anymore, at all."

"What are you saying, Randy?"

"I'm saying that if there's someone who wants to take her in, then both me and Kayleen would sign whatever papers it'd take."

"You've talked to Kayleen?"

"Yeah. I don't know where she is, though."

Colt let out a bitter laugh. "Of course, you don't."

"I don't. Seriously. She won't tell me. I called her about Sophie, and then I talked to her again when my friend told me about giving up your rights. He said it'd be no good if just I did it, so I asked Kayleen, and she said she'd do it too … if it means …"

"If it means that she'll be off the hook for the cost of raising her daughter?"

"Yeah. I know what you think. And you're right. We're a pair of losers. Only difference between us is that I don't mind admitting it. The only thing I can hang onto is that Sophie would be better off. Even you can't argue with me about that."

"No. I can't, and I won't. But I still don't get what you want me to do about it. I told you. It's Kelly you need to talk to, not me."

"You're involved, too. You know Sophie, and you know the system. You could help her."

Colt turned into the driveway at Cassie's place and brought the truck to a stop in the garage. "I'll have to talk to Kelly. I don't know the system that well."

"Will you do it then? Let me know what you find out?"

Colt blew out a sigh. "Let me make sure that I'm straight on what you want me to do?"

"I want you to find Sophie a family."

"And I've told you, it's not my place to do that. All I can do is pass on the information that you and Kayleen are willing to relinquish your parental rights if we can find her a family."

"It's not your job to find her a home, but I trust you, Colt. You'll do right by her. I'm not sure the system will, and before you say it, I know damned well that me and Kayleen haven't."

"You can say that again."

Randy was quiet for a few moments. "Will you see what you can do?"

Colt gripped the steering wheel tight and tipped his head back to look up through the sunroof. "I'll talk to Kelly."

"Thanks. I'll call you—"

"I'll call you when I have anything to say. Can I get you at this number?"

"Yeah. This is my cell. I always have it with me."

"Okay. I'll get back to you in a day or two."

"Thanks, Colt. You're the best hope Sophie's got."

He closed his eyes and blew out a big sigh when Randy hung up. Why had he gone and said that? He was Sophie's best hope? As if he wasn't too involved already! Randy wasn't stupid. He knew saying that would only add to Colt's sense of responsibility for the kid.

The door from the kitchen opened, and Cassie stood there, giving him a puzzled look. "Is everything okay?" she asked when he got out. "I thought I'd heard you come in but then I wasn't sure."

"Yeah. Sorry. I was on the phone."

"Oh. I'm sorry. I didn't mean to interrupt you."

"No. You didn't. It was Randy."

"Randy? Sophie's father? Is he back?"

Colt let out a bitter laugh as he followed her into the house. "No. And he doesn't plan on coming back either."

"What then?"

"He's trying to put me in charge of making sure Sophie finds a home here at the lake."

Cassie's eyes grew wide. "Why? How? That's not even in your power to do, is it?"

"No. It really isn't. But damn if he didn't make me feel like she's my responsibility." He went to the fridge and took out a beer. Cassie had bought him a six-pack, and it had sat in there untouched since he'd moved in. Tonight, he wanted a beer. He shot her an apologetic look. "Care to join me?"

She smiled. "Sure. We can take a cab in tonight if you still want to go."

"Yeah. I want to. I can't let him ruin our evening."

"I don't mind if you'd rather stay home."

He smiled and popped the tops off the bottles before handing her one. "I want to go. I want us to have a fun time with our friends. I want to put this out of my mind. I won't be able to do anything until I can talk to Kelly on Monday—and even then, I don't know that there's really anything I can do. I'm just a cop. There's a whole system in place to make sure the Sophies of this world are taken care of."

Cassie nodded. "But we both know that the system is overloaded."

Colt closed his eyes. She was right, of course.

"I'm sorry. I don't mean to pile it on you. But I feel responsible for her, too. I hate to think—"

"Then why don't we not think about it. Not until Monday?"

Cassie nodded. But he knew that it wouldn't be possible. Neither of them was the kind of person who could just switch off like that.

When the cab dropped them off in the square at the resort, Colt slid his arm around her shoulders as they walked toward the Boathouse.

"Sorry I was quiet on the way here. I promise I'll kick myself up the butt now."

She reached up and planted a peck on his lips. "There's no need to apologize. If I'm honest, I didn't even notice that you were quiet. I was lost in my own thoughts."

He blew out a sigh. "How about I call Kelly tomorrow? I know she won't mind. And neither of us will enjoy the weekend if we're just waiting and wondering."

Cassie smiled. "Okay, yes. That'd be good."

"Then that's what we'll do, but it means that we have to put it out of our minds for tonight. Deal?"

She nodded. "I can promise that I'll try."

"Yeah. Me, too." He held the door open for her to go in ahead of him.

"Hey, guys." Ivan greeted them when they got to the bar. "And how are you this evening?"

Colt smiled. "Good, thanks. How about you?"

Ivan grinned. "Great—in fact, I'm celebrating. Remember I told you about the backpacks campaign? Well, we hit our target two weeks early."

Cassie gave him a puzzled look. "Backpacks campaign?"

"Yeah. Did you know that when foster kids are moved, most of them only ever have garbage bags to put their clothes and things in? I know it might not sound like much, but having a backpack they can call their own is a big deal …"

Ivan carried on talking, Cassie was vaguely aware of what he was saying, but she couldn't focus on it. All she could think about was little Sophie. She could picture her with one arm in a cast and holding a black garbage bag in her other hand. Most of it was bunched up in her hand, empty because she had so few things to call her own. Cassie shot a glance at Colt, and he pursed his lips and gave her a slight nod.

Ivan stopped talking. "Did I say something wrong? I feel like I just put my foot in it with both of you, but I have no idea how."

"It's okay," said Colt. "It's not you. It's us."

Ivan laughed. "Now, it sounds like you're both breaking up with me."

Cassie smiled. "We wouldn't do that. You're awesome."

"No," agreed Colt. "It's just that there's a little girl on our minds tonight who's in that exact situation. And I don't think either of us thought about it before. About her having a few clothes stuffed in a garbage bag."

"Ah." Ivan looked crestfallen, and Cassie felt bad.

"Sorry. It shouldn't take away from you celebrating, though. You're doing great things with the fundraising. Helping lots of kids. That's wonderful."

"It is, but tell me about this little girl?"

Cassie looked at Colt. They'd agreed that they were going to try to put her out of their minds for tonight.

He shrugged. "Nah. Let's get a drink and celebrate with you instead. Where's Abbie?"

"She's gone on a little do-gooding mission."

Cassie laughed. "What do you mean?"

"Do you remember Neil, who I work with?"

"I think I've seen him around." Cassie seemed to remember that Abbie had gone out with Neil once, but she didn't want to bring that up.

"He doesn't come out much, and neither does his girlfriend, Merry. They're not really the sociable type. Abbie tried to get them to come out with everyone tonight, and they bailed at the last minute. So, she decided to buy them dinner and take it over to Merry's place."

Colt laughed. "That's right. Merry works at the library, and you two were instrumental in getting them together, right?"

Ivan nodded. "Yeah. They're good people. We keep trying to get them to come out with everyone, but at some point, I think we'll have to accept that it's just not their thing."

"We're all different," said Cassie. "I love that Abbie keeps trying to include them, though. She has talked about them at work. She's a sweetheart, isn't she?"

She loved the way Ivan smiled. "I obviously think so. In fact, I'm going to tell you two because I know you can keep secrets; I think she's ready to start wedding planning. I asked her at Christmas, and at first, she thought she wanted a long engagement. But I think now she's finding her feet, she's ready."

Colt slid his arm around Cassie's shoulders. "Must be something in the air."

Ivan's eyes grew wide, and he looked from Colt to Cassie and back again. "Anything you want to tell me?"

"Not quite yet," said Colt. "But watch this space."

Cassie smiled up at him. She'd told him she was ready and willing. She was happy to wait for him to choose his moment.

Zack appeared at Ivan's side. "Hey, guys. How is everyone?"

"Great, thanks," said Cassie. "How are you and Maria?"

"We're doing well, thanks."

"Where is she?" asked Colt.

"She should be here in a minute. My dad's coming to town next week, and she got some idea in her head that she wanted to pick something up for him." He shook his head. "I'm not sure I really understood what she was talking about. All I know is that she had to see someone at one of the stores before they close." He shrugged.

Cassie laughed. "Knowing Maria, it'll be some thoughtful little gift for your dad. I love her."

Zack smiled. "Funny you should mention that. I do, too."

"Any wedding bells sounding in your future?" asked Ivan.

Zack grinned. "This summer. We need to give our families enough notice. We're going to get married here, and they're coming from all over the country."

"That's great," said Colt. "Give your dad my regards, won't you?"

"Sure will. In fact, if you're out at all this week, I'm sure we'll run into you. He's not one to sit at home, so I'm sure we'll be all over town and doing the rounds meeting up with people."

"It's so nice that he's coming to visit," said Cassie. She wished her parents would come up to the lake, but these days they preferred her to go to them.

Zack grinned. "He loves it here. And you know he works with Eddie's dad? Well, these days, whenever Ted comes to see Eddie and April, Dad comes, too. He's in a hurry for us to get married because he wants to be a grandpa, like Ted."

Colt frowned. "Ted's a grandpa?"

"Maybe not by blood, but I wouldn't dare mention that fact to him."

Ivan looked puzzled. "Help me out? I'm not following."

"I can't blame you," said Colt. "I have trouble keeping up with everyone, and I've lived here my whole life. Okay. Zack's dad is Diego. He is partners with Eddie's dad, Ted."

"That's as far as I'm following. What about the grandpa bit?"

"Well," said Colt. "Eddie is married to April, who works at the bakery."

"No!" Zack shook his head vigorously. "Not yet. They've been together for a few years, but it took a long time for April's divorce to be finalized. They're engaged, but not married yet—that's another thing Ted wants to see happen."

"It's funny, I always think of them as married," said Colt.

"It sounds like they're as good as," said Ivan.

Cassie laughed. "I wouldn't let April hear you say that. I know she wants a big dream wedding."

Ivan laughed. "Of course. I should have known. Abbie wouldn't let me get away with saying that either."

"Anyway," Colt continued, "married or not, April's son Marcus thinks of Ted as his grandpa. And Ted has claimed Marcus as his grandson."

"He's not just claimed him," said Zack. "They made it official a while back. Eddie adopted Marcus as his son."

Cassie raised an eyebrow. "What about Marcus's father? How was Eddie able to adopt Marcus?"

Zack shrugged. "I don't know how it all when down, but Guy's in prison. There's a lot of bad blood there. He relinquished his parental rights."

Colt frowned. "How does that work?"

"Like I said, I don't really know the full story. I just know that Marcus calls Eddie Dad, and he calls Ted Grandpa. And when it came up in conversation, Eddie told me that as far as they and the law are concerned, Marcus is his son and Guy has no rights or responsibilities for him at all anymore."

Cassie looked at Colt, guessing that he was thinking about Sophie again.

Abbie and Maria arrived at that moment and joined them at the bar.

"What's going on?" asked Maria. "Why does everyone look so serious?"

"Yeah," agreed Abbie. "I thought we were celebrating."

Ivan smiled. "We are. We just got a bit off topic thinking about kids and parental rights."

Abbie looked at Cassie. "Is Sophie okay?"

"Yes. We weren't talking about her."

"Oh, sorry."

"Hey, kiddies!" Logan grinned around them as he joined the group. "What's happening? Are you coming to join us? Roxy's keeping us a table with Austin and the twins."

Cassie looked over, and Austin lifted a hand in greeting. He was sitting beside Amber and even from this distance, Cassie could tell that they were both uncomfortable. "We were just getting a drink."

"I'll get them. You go and sit down, if you like," said Colt.

"Thanks." She squeezed his hand before following Abbie and Maria over to join the others.

When they reached the table, Austin got up to leave.

"What's up? Do we smell bad or something?" asked Maria.

Austin laughed. "Not at all. It's just that all the guys are at the bar, and I'm guessing that you ladies will want to have your girly chat, so for your sake and mine, I'm going to join them."

Jade laughed. "You should stay. You might learn a thing or two."

Austin shook his head. "Thanks, but I'll pass."

Chapter Fifteen

Colt grasped Austin's shoulder when he got to the bar. "There you are. I thought maybe you were sticking close to Amber. How've you been?"

Austin made a face. "I've told you—"

Zack raised an eyebrow at him. "You've told us all a million times. Why don't you just ask her out?"

Austin blew out a sigh. "If I'd known that you were all going to harass me about it, I would have stayed next to her." He smiled. "She smells better than you do, and she doesn't give me any grief."

Colt laughed. "That's because you barely talk to her."

"Whatever. Can I get anyone a drink?"

"Nope." Colt handed him a beer. "I got you this. It's the least I could do. We haven't been out for a beer in way too long."

"And like I told Cassie, I know why, and it's fine by me. I'm happy for you."

"I know, but I miss you, bud."

"Aww," said Logan. "Isn't that sweet." He picked his drink up. "I'd rather canoodle with Roxy than listen to you two bromancing each other."

Zack smiled. "Yeah. Sorry guys, but I'm going back to Maria, too."

Ivan shrugged and laughed. "I don't want to be the third wheel. And sorry, but Abbie's much more attractive."

Colt watched them all go and then turned back to Austin. "So, how've you been?"

"Same as always. Nothing's changed in my world. More importantly, how've you been?"

Colt grinned. "Happier than I can remember. Well, I remember being happy before Cassie left, but this is different."

Austin smiled back at him. "This time it's for keeps?"

"Yep."

"Are you going to ask her to marry you?"

"I am." Colt met his gaze. "And I'm going to ask you to be my best man."

"You know it. That's been the deal since we were kids."

"It has. And I'll expect to be yours when the time comes."

Austin made a face. "That won't happen for a long time yet, but don't worry, I won't forget you."

"Don't leave it too long, will you? We're not getting any younger."

Austin laughed. "You were always the one who was in a hurry to settle down and have kids, not me. If it were up to you, you'd have a family of your own by now."

"I know. But at some point, you have to think that it might be too late."

"I don't think so. Wait. You're not trying to tell me something, are you?"

"What kind of something?"

"Cassie isn't …?"

Colt laughed. "No! But I can't wait until she is."

"You'd better hurry up and ask her to marry you then."

"I'm going to. Well, not hurry it. I want it to be right." He smiled. "I want it to be perfect."

"Knowing you, it will be."

"Anyway. Enough of the sappy stuff. Anything interesting happening with you?"

"Nothing really. Oh. That's not true. I meant to ask you what you know about Kayleen and Jimmy."

Colt blew out a sigh. "I can tell you that I'm sick of hearing their names, and Randy, too."

"Oh, that's right. I heard that Randy skipped town, too."

"Yep. Oh, wait. Kayleen was renting one of your places, wasn't she?"

"Yeah."

"Shit. I'm sorry."

"I'm not. Not really. I only let her have the place because she has that little girl, Sophie. And when I rented it to her, I didn't bank on Jimmy moving in with them. She knew I wouldn't throw them out because of Sophie, but …" He shook his head. "In another ten days or so, I'll be able to take the place back, the terms of the lease agreement will have been broken. So, it's probably all worked out for the best for me. I wish I could say the same for Sophie."

Colt took a drink of his beer.

"What's up?" asked Austin. "Did I say something wrong?"

"No. It's just that every time I turn around, Sophie's name comes up."

"I know you were on Jimmy's tail over Gramps' car. Were you involved with Kayleen and Sophie, too?"

"Not directly. I just had a hunch about what was going on there. Then Cassie got the proof of it when Sophie came in with a broken arm. It's Kelly Miles' area, not mine. But ... I don't know. I've felt something for that kid all along. And then tonight, get this, Randy called me to ask if I can help find her a home—like she's a stray puppy that needs rehoming."

Austin laughed. "Sorry. It's not funny. Just the way you describe it."

"Yeah, you can thank Kenzie for that one."

"So, what are you going to do?"

Colt shrugged. "I don't see that there's much I can do. Kelly's the one who finds families to place kids with."

Austin cocked his head to one side. "What about instead of finding a family, you volunteer to be one?"

"What?" The pulse pounded in his temples. "What are you saying?"

Austin held up his hand. "Ignore me. Sorry, that was a dumb thing to say. It was only because we'd been talking about you and Cassie and how if it were up to you, you'd already have a family by now. You two are going to be amazing parents, and that's what Sophie needs." He gave Colt an apologetic smile. "Sorry. I got carried away."

Colt stared at him. His mind was racing to match his pulse. It was a crazy idea! But now that Austin had planted it in his mind, he couldn't shake it.

"What? You're not taking me seriously, are you?"

Colt shrugged. "I don't know. I can't really, can I? I mean, Cassie and I are supposed to be starting our life together—starting a family of our own. How could I ask her to even think about it …" He shook his head. "It wouldn't work. We both have jobs. We don't work regular hours. We're not even married. They probably wouldn't consider us as suitable foster parents anyway. We couldn't go through the process quickly enough."

Austin was watching him closely.

"What?"

Austin smiled. "I'm not sure if I should say sorry or you're welcome for planting that idea in your head. But it's really taken root, hasn't it?"

Colt nodded. "It shouldn't, but it has."

"Do you think you need to talk to Cassie about it?"

Colt looked over to where she was sitting chatting with the others. Would it be fair to her to even bring it up? He shook his head slowly. "I don't know, bud. I just don't know."

~ ~ ~

It was a wonderful evening. Cassie enjoyed spending time with their friends in a way that she hadn't been able to since she'd come back to the lake. She'd felt so uncomfortable. She'd spent her time determinedly avoiding Colt, and that had made her feel closed off. She hadn't been open with the girls because she'd known that if she opened up even a little bit, she wouldn't be able to stop the truth from pouring out—the truth that she was still in love with him.

She smiled as she watched him talking with Luke and Zack. He was such a great guy. She knew how lucky she was. He turned and caught her eye and excused himself from the conversation to come over to her.

"I was only looking," she told him. "You didn't need to leave them."

He looked down into her eyes and sent shivers racing down her spine. "Why would I want to stand around talking with them when I could be dancing with you?"

"Dancing?" She raised an eyebrow.

"Yes. Do you want to?"

She looked up at the band who had just started to play a slow ballad. She chuckled. "Dancing can lead to other things, you know."

He laughed. "That's what I'm hoping."

Once they were out on the dance floor, he held her close, and she rested her head against his shoulder. This felt like coming home—she smiled to herself—and like Homecoming. It was years ago, but she remembered it like it was yesterday. His arms tightened around her and she looked up.

"Are you remembering all the times we've danced, too?"

She smiled. "Homecoming."

"You were my queen. You still are."

She chuckled. She hadn't been the kind of girl who would have wanted to be Homecoming Queen. But he'd made her feel as special as if she were. She reached up and kissed his lips. "You are the best person I've ever known."

He smiled, but there was something in his eyes that worried her. She rested her head back on his shoulder, not wanting to spoil the moment by asking him what it was. He was tense, though, and now that she was paying attention, she could feel his heart hammering in his chest.

She looked up again. "Is there something on your mind?"

She expected him to smile and reassure her that he was fine. Instead, he pursed his lips and nodded. "I'm sorry, Cass. I'm a little preoccupied, I guess."

"Want to tell me about it?"

"Can you wait till we get home?"

She nodded. She wanted to put it out of her mind and just enjoy this moment, back in his arms, dancing with him like they were always supposed to have been.

She gave him a rueful smile. "Sophie?"

He nodded.

"Me, too. I can't get her out of my mind. I can see her little face as she carries a garbage bag of her things." She shook her head. "I wish there was something we could do."

Colt held her gaze for a long moment. "Would you want to do it if there was?"

She gave him a puzzled look. "I thought that's what I just said."

"Wishing you could and seeing it through when you can … they're two very different things."

"What do you mean?"

He shook his head. "Sorry. It can wait."

She took his hand and led him off the dance floor. "I can't wait. I want to know what you mean, and I want to hear about what you're thinking. What do you say, do you want to call it a night?"

He stopped at the edge of the dance floor. "Are you sure? I don't want to spoil our night."

"You're not spoiling it. We're just deciding to take it in a different direction."

He smiled. "You always knew how to spin things to the positive."

"I just prefer to look on the bright side. Come on, let's say goodnight to everyone. If we go now, we won't have to wait in line for a cab."

~ ~ ~

Colt paid the cab driver and watched him pull away while Cassie unlocked the front door to let them in. He was second-guessing himself. This was a crazy idea. He had no right to even suggest to Cassie that they might take Sophie in themselves. That was no way to start their life together. His idea of their future saw them getting married and starting a family, sure, but a family comprised of kids of their own—of babies they made together. He turned when she spoke.

"Are you coming in?"

"Sorry."

She came to him and slid his arms up around his neck. "I don't mind standing here with you admiring the stars if that's what you want." Her expression sobered. "But that's not what you're doing, is it? Let's go in, and you can tell me what's on your mind. You're starting to worry me."

He tightened his arms around her waist. "That's the last thing I want to do, love. I'm questioning myself is all. Wondering if I should forget the idea."

She planted a kiss on his lips. "How about you tell me what it is, and then, we can decide together if it's something we want to forget?"

"Okay." He followed her though to the kitchen. "Do you feel like a brandy?"

"Sure. Do you want to take it outside?"

He nodded.

"You pour the drinks. I'll go get the blankies."

He met her out on the deck overlooking the lake. There was no moon tonight. He waited for her to get comfortable on the sofa underneath the blanket then snuggled in beside her. He handed her a glass.

She smiled. "These things always tickle me."

"The name?"

"Yes. A snifter. I love that. Or a balloon."

He nodded.

"Sorry." She looked up into his eyes. "I was hoping to lighten the mood, but you're not feeling very light, are you?"

"No." He held her gaze for a long moment and decided that the best thing to do was to just spit it out. "This is probably going to sound crazy—because it is. But ..."

"But what?"

"Well ..." He wanted to give her some context, tell her about Eddie adopting Marcus and how Austin had planted the idea in his mind, but none of it was relevant, really. "It's about Sophie."

"I know."

He couldn't figure out the expression on her face. She looked uncomfortable, wary. He wasn't used to that from her.

She sucked in a deep breath and then slowly blew it out. "Can I say something first?"

"Sure." Perhaps whatever she had to say would mean there was no point in him bringing up the possibility of them taking Sophie in themselves.

She almost looked as if she was in pain when she spoke again. "I know that it's a ridiculous idea, but ... do you think there's any chance ... would you want ..."

He smiled around the lump in his throat and blinked away the pricking feeling in his eyes. "Are you about to ask me if we should take her?"

Her eyes widened. "I'm sorry! I know it's crazy,"

"You're only as crazy as I am. That's what I was building up to asking you."

"You were?!"

"Yep. It seemed as though every conversation I had tonight was trying to point me in that direction, and then, Austin just came flat out and said it."

She pressed her lips together, but he could tell she was smiling.

"What made you go there?"

She shrugged. "For me, it was Ivan talking about garbage bags. I just keep thinking about her—seeing her standing there with her whole life not even filling half a bag. She deserves so much more—every kid deserves so much more than that."

"They do. And that's what I kept trying to tell myself. There are so many kids in that situation; I can't save them all. The way I can help is by doing my job. But …" He shook his head. "It's not enough. Sophie's so much closer to home."

"And even though we can't save them all, we can save her. She's such a bright little thing. She deserves a good life, and we could give her that. I know we could."

He held her gaze. "But what about us? What about the kids that we want to have?"

"I know what you mean. And I'm not naïve. I know Sophie could be a real challenge, but …" she smiled. "I think it'd be worth it, don't you?"

"I do."

"So, are we agreed?"

He shook his head. "I think we need to take some time to think about it first. It's a huge commitment." He took hold of her hand under the blanket and squeezed it tight. "And there are practical details to consider, too. I don't know how the whole process works. I don't know if they'd even consider us suitable. We're not even married yet."

He loved her all the more when she smiled. "Not to sound too pragmatic, but we both know that we want to be married, and I'm not one of those girls who wants or needs a big wedding. We can take care of that quickly if we need to."

He touched her cheek. "No. We have to do what's right for us. If we do this, we can't put Sophie's needs ahead of our own. I want you to have the wedding, the big deal, not to rush it out of the way as a detail to be taken care of."

"The way I understand it, being a parent means that you do put your kids' needs ahead of your own." She smiled. "And I don't mind if that's what it takes."

"We don't know what it will take yet. We need to talk to Kelly and see if it's even possible. But first, I really do think we each need to take some time and think about it—be sure that this is what we want. We don't want to dive in out of enthusiasm and then discover that we've bitten off more than we can chew. You are most important to me, Cass. We've waited all this time. I don't want to screw things up for us now."

She nodded. "I know. You're right. There's a lot to think about. It would change everything." She stared out at the lake and then looked back at him. "There are all kinds of practical details. So many ways it would change our lives."

He was starting to think that she was already talking herself out of it.

She smiled. "But, to me, at least, it feels like the right thing to do. It really does. If things had gone differently between us, we might have had a seven-year-old girl of our own by now."

He smiled. "I've thought that. Maybe she was supposed to be with us, but she's been living a different life until we finally got our act together."

Cassie's smile faded. "When you put it like that, it makes me want to hurry up and get to the day when we can bring her home. Like it's time for her to get started on the life she's meant to live, just like we are."

He slid his arm around her shoulders and hugged her to him. "Let's sleep on it and see how we feel in the morning."

"Okay. But I think we already know, don't we?"

"Yeah. I think we do."

Chapter Sixteen

Cassie brought the car to a stop at the mailbox when she got home. It'd been a long day. Mondays always were. But today had seemed especially so. She'd had trouble concentrating this morning. Colt was going to talk to Kelly Miles—just to get an initial idea of whether them taking Sophie was even a possibility. He'd texted her at eleven to let her know that he wouldn't have any news for her today, though. Kelly was in court and was expected to be there all day.

Cassie got out of the car to get the mail. She looked up at the sight of headlights coming around the corner from the top end of the lake and frowned when the vehicle slowed.

"Cassie!"

She smiled when she saw Emma Douglas roll down her window. No. she was Emma Benson these days.

"How are you? I've been meaning to catch up with you."

"I'm great, thanks; how are you?"

"We're all doing great, thanks." Emma smiled happily. "I'm so glad you're back here, and that you and Colt are back together. I'm so happy for you."

"Thanks. I'm pretty thrilled myself."

"I'll bet you are. You two belong together. Has he popped the question yet? Are you getting married?"

Cassie laughed. "Not yet, but we have talked about it."

"Oh, I hope you'll have an engagement party. You should. And do it soon. We could do with a party around here to get everyone together. I feel as though I haven't been out with everyone in ages."

"Aww, you should get Jack to bring you to the Boathouse. Are you going to the Valentine's dinner?"

"Oh, yes. I'd forgotten about that. We'll be there on Saturday. It seems like the only time we go anywhere lately is to Holly's when all the kids come over. She said you and Colt might come ... do you think you'll make it this week?"

"Maybe. It all depends on how late he has to work."

"Of course. Do you think you'll be bringing kiddies of your own any time soon?"

Cassie's heart beat a little faster at the question. Maybe they would.

Emma raised her eyebrows. "What does that look mean? I only meant are you two going to be starting a family any time soon? I know Colt always wanted kids. Oh, wait ... you're not ... pregnant, are you?" Her eyes widened.

"No! It's not that." All of a sudden, Cassie wanted to talk. She wanted to share what she was feeling and to get some friendly advice. "Are you in a hurry to get home?"

"No. I'm on my way back from Charlie's. She's been working on my website. Jack's picking Isabel up from his mom's, and they won't be back for a while yet."

"Do you want to come in for a little while?"

"I'd love to."

Emma followed her to the house and parked outside.

In the kitchen, Cassie offered her a soda. "Thanks, Em. Do you mind if I run something by you?"

"Of course. You can tell me anything. You know I'd never breathe a word."

Cassie smiled. She'd forgotten how sweet Emma was.

"Is it about having kids?"

"Kind of. This will probably sound crazy to you, but Colt and I are thinking about taking in little Sophie Wilson. Do you know her?"

"I do. Poor little thing. I can't believe Kayleen would just abandon her like that. I never did like her, but to think of leaving your own daughter behind." She shuddered. "Sorry. I thought Sophie was with the Murrays. They're nice people."

"They are, but it's only a temporary placement."

Emma set her glass down. "And you're not talking about temporary?"

Cassie shook her head.

"Wow!"

"Is that a good wow, or a you think we must be crazy, wow?"

Emma laughed. "It's an I think that's amazing, wow!" Her smile faded. "But I'm an idealist, and I believe in fairy tales, or at least that's what Jack would tell you. What about the reality? You two have only just gotten back together. Don't you want time to just be with each other ... and to have your own kids?"

"We do, but can't we do both?"

"I suppose? But are you sure you're ready to turn your lives upside down for a little girl? She seems like a sweet little thing, but after all that she's been through, you don't know what problems she might have. She might be a real handful."

"I'm sure she will be. Like you say, after everything she's been through ... but doesn't she deserve someone to love her? Doesn't she deserve to be part of a family where she won't have to go through any more horrible things? With us, she'd have a stable life. She'd know that she's loved and ..." Cassie stopped herself. "Am I being too idealistic? I don't know what it's like to live the kind of life Sophie has. My childhood was idyllic. So was Colt's."

Emma smiled at her. "You've always been realistic. You've always known what you want and found a way to get it. You've worked hard and put in the effort to get to where you want to be in life. I don't see any reason you wouldn't do that with Sophie, too. You're not looking at it through rose-colored glasses. I'd say if anyone could make it work, it's you and Colt. My biggest question is, are you sure it's what you want—for yourselves? I know you want it for Sophie, but is it right for the two of you? Having a child changes the way you live. Have you thought what it would look like on an everyday basis? Take tonight, for example. It's after seven. You're just getting home from work. Colt's not even finished yet. What would that mean for Sophie?"

Cassie nodded. "I know. I've been thinking about that. There are a couple of people in town who watch kids after school. And I don't have to work late. I only do it on Mondays to help out people who work. I could change my late days so that they coincide with Colt's early days. We could make it work."

"I know you could if you want to. I just want to make sure that you've thought about the angles."

"I've thought about nothing else for the last few days."

Emma smiled. "I'd guess that you could give it a trial run? Maybe Sophie could come and stay with you guys for a couple of weeks to see how it works, see how you all feel about it. You don't have to make the big commitment to it being a permanent arrangement straightaway, do you? Or do you?"

"We don't even know if it's a real possibility, yet. I just wanted to talk to someone. Someone other than Colt. We've gone over it and over it."

"Well, you know I'm always here for you. Anytime."

They both turned at the sound of Colt's truck pulling into the garage.

Emma finished her soda and took the glass to the sink. "You know where I am if you want to talk some more. I need to get going, though."

"You don't have to leave just because he's home."

"I know. It's because it reminded me that Jack and Isabel will be home soon." She came and gave Cassie a hug. "You'll make the right decision. I know you will. Call me anytime. And if you don't, I'll call you."

Colt came in from the garage. "Hey, Em. It's good to see you."

"You, too. But I'm just leaving."

"You don't have to."

"I really do." She smiled. "But I'll see you both soon. Don't worry. I'll see myself out."

They watched her go, then Colt came to Cassie and wrapped her in a hug. "What's with Emma?"

"Nothing. I ran into her at the mailbox and asked her if she wanted to come in for a while. I like her a lot."

"Yeah. She's awesome." He smiled. "I'm glad she didn't stick around, though. I brought us take-out for dinner. I didn't want to bring it in in case she was joining us and you were already making something."

Cassie laughed. "Aww. Well, go get it. Take-out is perfect. I was late getting home myself, and then with Emma coming in, it's getting late."

They sat side by side at the island to eat. "How was your day?"

"Honestly? Long, and I was distracted for most of it."

Colt nodded. "About the same as mine then. I was all psyched up to talk to Kelly this morning. Then when I heard she was in court for the day ..." He sighed. "I hope I'll hear from her tomorrow."

"I do, too. I keep remembering that she might just say no, this isn't even an option."

"I know. I keep thinking about that, too. I don't want to get too caught up in it in case she just says a flat no."

"Do you think that's likely?"

"I don't think Kelly would tell us no if it were up to her. But I don't know what all the rules are around it."

"Well, we'll just have to wait until tomorrow and hope that she can answer your questions then."

"If she says it's a possibility, we should both sit down with her to talk about it. When would be a good time for you?"

Cassie shrugged. "I don't know. I'll have to shuffle patients around to fit with whenever Kelly can make it." She held his gaze for a moment.

"What?"

"If we get Sophie, we're both going to have to try to work some flexibility into our schedules."

"I know. I almost talked to Don about it today. But I held back. I don't want to go telling folks that we're even thinking about it. There's no point if Kelly says it's a no-go, is there?"

Cassie lowered her eyes to her food.

He chuckled beside her. "You're so transparent, Dr. Stevens. Who did you talk to? Was it Em?"

She gave him a guilty smile. "Yeah. I'm sorry. It just hit me when I saw her. I needed someone to tell me that I'm not crazy to even consider it."

"Hey, don't apologize. I understand. I already talked about it with Austin when it first came up. I get it. I wasn't saying that we shouldn't talk to people. Just that, well, to be honest, I held back from talking to Don because I didn't want to get his hopes up. He and Mary both know Sophie, and they'd take her themselves if they were younger."

"Oh, I can see that. They're wonderful parents. All their kids are lovely people."

"They are, but they're also parents themselves—to kids Sophie's age. Much as Don and Mary would love to take her, they're more like her grandparents than parents."

"True. Well, if she can come with us, they'll be like honorary grandparents to her, I'm sure."

Colt smiled. "I know they'd love that. It makes me think, though. I need to talk to my folks. I don't know how they'll feel about it."

"I think they'll love the idea."

He nodded. "You're probably right. What about yours?"

Cassie made a face. "They could go either way. I don't imagine they'll be thrilled at the idea, but if we can make it happen, I know they'll be supportive—after they've grumbled for a while."

"Yeah. That sounds about right. But, until we talk to Kelly, it's all just conjecture."

Colt was sitting at his desk the next morning when his cell phone rang.

"Deputy Stevens," he answered.

"Hi, Colt. It's Kelly. Sorry I didn't get back to you yesterday. It was one of those days."

"No problem. If anyone understands how that goes, I do."

"I'm sure. What can I do for you?"

Colt looked around. He didn't really want to explain with other people around. "Can I buy you lunch?"

"Hmm. Interesting offer. Does this mean it's pleasure and not business?"

He chuckled. "It's both. You know I consider your company a pleasure. But I do need to talk to you about something."

"Something work related?"

"It's related to your work and very personal for me."

"Now, I am intrigued. I'm slammed this morning. What about twelve-thirty at the Boathouse? I can give you an hour then."

"That's great. Thanks. How do you feel about Giuseppe's? It's closer to your office."

"And more private."

He had to laugh. "There's no fooling you, is there?"

"I like to think not. Do you want to give me a clue what this is about?"

Colt looked around and then said. "Sophie."

"Wilson?"

"Yeah."

Kelly was quiet for a long moment. "I'll see you at twelve-thirty. One question."

"Fire away."

"Will Cassie be there, too?"

He thought about it. "Maybe." He was fairly certain that she might be able to get away from work for at least half an hour at lunch time.

"Good. I'll see you then."

He left the office at twelve fifteen. It wasn't far to Giuseppe's, but he wanted to be there in case Cassie or Kelly—or both—showed up early.

He'd called Cassie to let her know, and she'd said she had a break between patients from twelve-fifteen to one-fifteen, which could work out perfectly if Kelly was on time.

He was pleased to see both their cars already in the small parking lot behind the building when he pulled in. He went inside and found them sitting at a corner booth. They already had drinks, and there was a soda waiting for him.

He slid in beside Cassie and pecked her cheek. "I'm glad I came early. Thanks for this, Kelly."

Kelly smiled. "I'm intrigued. Though, I have a sneaking suspicion I know what you want to talk to me about."

"You do?" Cassie looked surprised.

"You want to know if the two of you can take Sophie in, don't you?"

"We do. But how did you know?" asked Colt.

She laughed. "I know you both. I've seen the way you each reacted to Sophie and her story. I know what kind of people you are. I mean, come on … the doctor and the deputy. Two people who care about the community they serve. It's not a huge leap to understand that you might care enough about a kid like Sophie to want to take her in."

"And …?" Colt's heart was racing in his chest. He could feel his pulse pounding in his temples. From the way Cassie was crushing his fingers, he knew she was just as nervous about what Kelly might say as he was.

Kelly blew out a sigh. "I admire the sentiment. But there are a lot of realities that will probably make it impossible. And I'm only talking about the way things work. I'm not even going to touch on what it would mean for the two of you and your relationship and the future Stevens kidlets that I assume you plan on having."

"What are the obstacles?" asked Cassie.

"For starters, the court's preference is to keep a child with family wherever possible."

"But all her family have abandoned her!" Colt was surprised at Cassie's tone. It was partly indignant and partly pleading.

"Not all of them. Her parents, yes, but there are aunts and grandparents."

Colt scowled. "You're not seriously telling me that the court would place her with them?" He knew that Kayleen's father lived out of town, in a cabin on the way up to Stanton Falls. And Randy's sister occasionally came through town. He couldn't think of any other relatives, and he was fairly sure that if there were any, he would have encountered them through his work.

Kelly shrugged. "My point is that they would want to explore all those options first. It's complicated with Randy and Kayleen being gone. That means the state is responsible for her, and though the state has her best interests at heart, it's bound up in its own rules and red tape."

Colt met her gaze. "That was something I needed to tell you. Randy called me. Both he and Kayleen are looking to offload her—or at least offload any financial obligations toward her.

He told me that they're both willing to relinquish their parental rights."

"Hmm." Kelly didn't say anything, waiting while the server set a pizza and three plates down on the table. When he'd gone, she nodded slowly. "That makes it a whole different matter."

"How?" Cassie asked eagerly. "Does it help somehow?"

"It might. If you're serious about this and they're willing to assign you guardianship …"

"How does that work?" asked Colt.

Kelly's eyebrows knit together. "I'm not sure we should even talk about it yet. Just know that it's an option. But first, you need to be fully aware of what you'd be letting yourselves in for. All you've seen is a sweet little kid who's been through hell and you want to help. That's very different from taking a troubled little girl into your home and committing to raise her. Fairy tale happy endings are few and far between in this line of work."

Colt nodded. "We know that."

"Knowing it and living through it are two very different matters, Colt. I'm not just thinking about Sophie here. I consider the two of you to be my friends. You're at the beginning of your lives together. I'd hate to see that get screwed up by issues you don't even see coming—and that you really don't have to take on."

"And we appreciate it," said Cassie. "But we've talked about it, and we know we want to do this."

Colt couldn't help smiling to himself. He'd believed that he was more committed to this idea than Cassie was; he'd worried a little that perhaps she was doing it just for him. Hearing her talk to Kelly made it clear that she was just as invested as he was.

Kelly looked thoughtful as she served herself a slice of pizza. "How about this …" She set her fork down and looked at them. "Sophie's going to have to leave the Murrays next Monday. I haven't found a family placement that can take her. It's looking like group is the only available option. I don't like that for her, and the judge assigned to her case is big on keeping the younger kids out of group homes wherever possible. I could propose that Sophie come stay with the two of you as an interim placement."

Cassie frowned. "We don't want to be an interim measure."

Kelly held up her hand. "I know. But I can't propose you as fosters, you're not even in the system. Doing it this way would achieve a few things. Most importantly, it'd give you the chance to experience what it's really like to have her in your home. And if you find that you do want to commit for the long haul, it also gives us time to get Kayleen and Randy to assign guardianship to you. That'll be so much faster than trying to get you vetted, trained, and approved."

Colt nodded. That made sense.

"So, what do you say? Do you want me to ask the court if I can place her with you for two weeks starting next Monday?"

"Do you think the judge will allow it?" asked Colt.

"Yeah. I do. Once I explain the circumstances, I think she'll agree to it."

"Great." Cassie smiled. "Then, yes." She turned to Colt. "We can, can't we?"

He nodded. "We sure can."

Kelly grinned. "There are still a lot of hurdles to overcome, but I can tell you, I have a good feeling about this."

Colt smiled at her. "I do, too. Thanks, Kelly."

She looked thoughtful, and Colt's heart sank. "What? Is there a problem?"

"No. Can you both be at home on Friday after school?"

Colt exchanged a glance with Cassie. He knew that her first instinct was to say no—the same as him. But this was a telling moment. If they were going to do this, then Sophie would have to become a priority, too.

Cassie nodded. "I can make it work. What time?"

"I could bring her up to your place at four."

"I'll talk to Don and make sure I'm home."

Kelly smiled. "Great. We have ourselves a date. I'll bring Sophie out to your place at four and pick her up at eight."

Colt couldn't hide his smile. Neither could Cassie as she squeezed his hand even tighter and nodded happily at Kelly.

Chapter Seventeen

On Friday afternoon, Cassie typed up her notes after her last appointment of the day and shut down her computer. Her hands were shaking as she gathered her things into her purse. This was the first time since she'd been here that she'd rescheduled patient appointments. It didn't feel comfortable. She prided herself on being dependable. But today was different. Heck, the rest of her life would be different if Sophie came to live with them.

She got to her feet. She'd still be her dependable self, though. But her priority would be that Sophie could depend on her.

She jumped when her office door opened, and Abbie popped her head in with a smile. "Oh, you *are* on your way out, then."

Cassie checked her watch. "Why? What's wrong."

"Nothing. Don't look like that. I'm not going to ask you to stay to see someone. I was wondering why you hadn't left yet. You don't want to be late getting home."

Cassie smiled. "Thanks. No, I don't."

"Relax. It's going to be great. I know you're nervous, but I'll bet Sophie's even more nervous."

"Probably." Just realizing that helped Cassie. After all, this was about Sophie. It was about making her feel welcome.

"And don't forget," added Abbie. "This visit is as much for you and Colt as it is for her. You need to know that you're going to be comfortable with it all, and with her."

"Thanks." Cassie shifted her purse strap higher on her shoulder. "I should go, shouldn't I?"

Abbie laughed. "Yes. And don't forget to breathe on the way. You'll be no use to anyone if you forget to do that."

Cassie smiled. "Thanks, Abbie."

"It's going to be great. You'll see. I'm not in tomorrow morning, but call me if you want someone to talk to, okay?"

"Thanks. I might."

"And, if not, then I guess we'll see you tomorrow night."

Cassie frowned.

"The Valentine's dinner. You said you're going, didn't you?"

"Oh. Yes."

Abbie laughed. "Just go. You can only focus on one thing at a time. Get on home—and enjoy it. If this all works out the way you think, then this first visit will be a day you'll always remember. Have some fun with her, make it a good memory."

"Aww." Tears pricked behind Cassie's eyes. "Thanks, Abbie."

"Stop thanking me and get out of here, would you?"

Cassie was relieved to see that the driveway was empty, and the garage door was still closed when she got home. She was the first here. She parked in the garage and hurried into the kitchen. She had snacks and fruit in the fridge for Sophie. She looked around. Everywhere was neat and tidy. She hoped it would look inviting and not intimidating. She didn't know what Sophie was used to.

She went to the door to the garage when she heard Colt's truck. He looked so handsome when he got out and smiled at her. "Hey. We both made it on time."

"Yes. I was worried Kelly might be here before us."

He came to her and wrapped her in a hug. "Are you okay?"

She nodded. "I'm a bit jittery."

He raised an eyebrow.

"Nervous," she explained. "Aren't you? I want this to go well."

"Yeah. I am a little nervous. I hope she'll feel comfortable with us."

"I hope she'll like the house."

Colt laughed. "She'll think it's a freaking palace."

"That's kind of what I mean. I know they were living in one of Austin's cheaper rentals. This place will be a bit different for her."

Colt shrugged. "My guess is that she'll love it. And we have to remember that she's just a kid. She's not going to have the same hang-ups that grown-ups do—that we do."

"I suppose. Oh. It sounds like they're here. Come on. Let's go out front." She took his hand and led him through the house to the front door. Her heart was racing as she opened it.

Kelly got out of her car and let Sophie out. "Hi, guys. Here we are."

"Hi, Kelly. Hello, Sophie."

Sophie smiled and came to them. "Hi, Dr. Stevens. Hi, Deputy Stevens."

Kelly gave Cassie an odd look.

"What's wrong?"

Kelly laughed. "Don't look so worried. It just never occurred to me before that you're already a Stevens."

Cassie smiled. "Yes. It's my name, too."

Kelly smirked. "Well, isn't that handy."

"I like to think so," said Colt. He turned to Sophie. "Do you want to come in?"

Sophie looked around. "Yes, please."

Cassie led them to the living room, and once they were all seated, she smiled around at them. "Does anyone want a drink?"

"I don't have time," said Kelly. "I want to make sure that the three of you are okay, and then I need to get back into town. I have a few things to do before I come to collect Sophie at eight."

"We can bring her if that would make life easier," said Colt.

"Thanks, but I need to do it. Why don't we get started?"

Colt reached out and took hold of Cassie's hand. Sophie smiled to herself as she watched them.

"Sounds good to me," said Colt. He winked at Sophie. "What are we getting started on?"

"Well," said Kelly. "I need to be sure that you all understand what's going on here, and I'd like to answer any questions you might have."

"I know what's happening," said Sophie.

"Do you want to explain it to them?" asked Kelly.

"Okay." She smiled at Cassie and then at Colt. "I don't have a family anymore. My daddy's worthless—"

Cassie sputtered, but Kelly shot her a warning look to let Sophie continue uninterrupted.

Sophie smiled. "That's what Mommy says. But Jimmy says she is, too. But it doesn't matter now anyway. You see, Mommy left town with Jimmy and Daddy left, too." She picked up a cushion from the sofa and held it in her lap.

"None of them wanted to take me with them," she added in a matter-of-fact tone. She met Cassie's gaze. "Miss Miles has to find me a new family. That's her job, you see."

Cassie nodded, wanting nothing more than to go to her and wrap her up in a hug.

"She wants to know if I get along with you guys, that's why I'm here."

"And how do you feel about being here?" asked Kelly.

Sophie shrugged. "I told you there's no point."

Cassie's heart sank. In all the talking and fretting that she and Colt had been doing, it hadn't occurred to them that perhaps Sophie wouldn't want to live with them.

"Remind me why?" asked Kelly.

Sophie shrugged again.

"Don't you want to give them a chance?" Kelly pushed.

Cassie wondered if this was Kelly's way of making them see that this wasn't going to work. She'd guess that Colt was thinking the same thing judging by the way he was gripping her hand so tightly.

Sophie clutched the cushion tighter and rubbed her chin against her shoulder before she answered. She looked up, first at Cassie, then at Colt. "Because you two are nice, and I'm just trash. All I do is get in the way."

Cassie bit down on her bottom lip at the same time that Colt crushed her fingers.

"Why do you say that?" asked Kelly.

"Because that's what Jimmy always said. I thought maybe he was just mean. But then Dakota at school said I'm trash too."

Cassie couldn't hold back any longer. She went to sit beside Sophie and put her arm around her shoulders.

Sophie looked up at her. She didn't seem upset. She was simply repeating what she'd been told—as if it was true.

"Sweetheart, that's not true. You are not trash. They just said that to be mean."

"You're kind."

"I try to be, but I'm not saying this to be kind. I'm telling you the truth. You are a very good, very bright person." Sophie didn't look impressed, and Cassie looked at Colt to help her.

He came to sit on the other side of Sophie, and she looked up at him.

"Cassie's right, you know. Do you want to know how I can prove it?"

She nodded. "I knew you could prove things. Jimmy said you couldn't prove nothing."

Colt smiled. "Well, he was wrong about that, wasn't he?"

"Was he?"

"He sure was. I proved that he had done some bad things."

"Is that why they left?"

Cassie held her breath. Was Colt going to admit to her that he was a big part of the reason that her mom and Jimmy had left town? Would she hold it against them if he did?

Colt nodded slowly. Of course, he was going to be truthful with her. "I think so. Jimmy knew that he was going to be in trouble, so he ran away."

Sophie nodded. "And Mommy went with him." She picked at the fabric of the pillow, then looked up. "Thank you."

Colt cocked his head to one side.

"I made a wish that they'd both leave here and that I wouldn't have to go with them." She smiled. "My wish came true."

Colt smiled. "You're welcome. But do you mind if I tell you something?"

"What's that?"

"I feel kind of responsible for you not having a family anymore."

"It's not your fault."

"I know, but Cassie and I, we're hoping that you might want to be part of our family. Do you want to get to know us a bit better to see if you'd like that?"

Two lines furrowed her little brow.

Cassie glanced at Kelly, but she shook her head, indicating they should wait for Sophie to speak.

Eventually, she looked up. "I'd like it a lot, but ..."

"But what?" asked Cassie.

"But ..." She shrugged. "I don't know."

"Well, since you don't know," said Kelly, "how about we all take a little time to figure it out? You can visit this evening, and then I'll take you back to the Murrays. If you all want more time together, I can bring you back on Monday, and you can stay for two weeks."

Sophie smiled. "I'd like that."

"Great." Kelly got to her feet. "I'll leave you to it. I'll be back at eight."

"Would you like a drink, Sophie?" asked Cassie.

"Yes, please."

"Come in the kitchen with me, then."

Colt watched them go before he walked Kelly out to her car. "What do you think?" he asked.

"I think this could be great for all of you. I did that because I want you both to understand where she is. She thinks that she's disposable. And I need you and Cassie to think long and hard about what you're doing here. At the moment, Sophie doesn't even think she's worthy of coming to live with you guys. If she does, I'd like to think it'll be for good."

"Of course. We're not just toying with the idea, Kelly. We're committed to it."

Kelly opened her car door. "I know." She smiled. "Sorry. If I'm honest, I think this is the perfect match. I'm thrilled that Sophie could get so lucky. But at the same time, this job makes you cynical after a while; if something seems too good to be true, it usually is. My number one task is to find these kids homes, but in my heart, it's to try and protect them from further pain."

Colt nodded. He understood where she was coming from. "I know I can't reassure you with words. They're not enough. But we'll prove it to you. You'll see."

Kelly laughed. "I have a feeling you will. But I have to go. I'll see you at eight."

Colt took a moment before he went back inside. He understood that he couldn't even imagine how Sophie felt. His childhood had been idyllic compared to hers. His parents had raised him and his brother. They hadn't had a lot of money, but they'd always had enough. More importantly, he'd always known that he was loved—that his parents were there for him and always would be. They still were. They spent their winters in Mexico these days, but they'd be back in the spring. He smiled. They'd bought one of the condos over at Four Mile a couple of years ago, and he'd bought the house from them. Over the summer, they'd come out here for barbecues on the weekends. They loved Cassie and had been thrilled to hear that they were back together. He knew that they'd love Sophie, too, and treat her as their own.

But that would all be new to Sophie. She wasn't used to being included in family gatherings. He hated to think about what she was used to. He went back inside, promising himself as he went that he would do everything in his power to make sure that in the future, she'd learn all about what love and family and belonging meant.

He stopped in the doorway to the kitchen. Sophie was sitting on one of the stools at the island, and Cassie was standing next to her, pouring her a glass of milk. His heart clenched in his chest at the sight of them. He'd wanted to be a husband and a father ever since he could remember. He'd never pictured it like this, but at that moment, he knew that they were his family.

"And it really comes from cows?" Sophie's expression was comical.

Cassie nodded. "It really does. Maybe one weekend we can take a drive out to the dairy farm, and you can learn all about it."

Sophie held up her glass and squinted at it. "Is it cow pee?"

Colt laughed, and they both turned to look at him.

"No. It's not pee," he said as he went in to join them. "It's what mother cows produce to feed their calves."

"What's a calve?"

"A baby cow," said Colt.

"And when there's just one, it's called a calf, but when there's more than one, we say calves," explained Cassie.

Sophie nodded, looking skeptical. She took a big gulp of the milk and then set the glass down with a big smile on her face.

"I like it. It's better than soda. We have it at school, but Mommy never bought it. She got us soda."

Colt shot a glance at Cassie. He knew that, if nothing else, Sophie's diet would improve when she came to live with them.

"So, ladies, what do we want to do?"

Sophie shrugged. "Do you have a TV?"

"We do. Do you want to watch it?" Colt had hoped that she might want to do something else, but it was most important that she should feel comfortable.

"I can sit and watch it and be quiet."

Colt closed his eyes. Of course, that was no doubt what she was used to hearing. "You can if you want to, but Cassie and I were thinking about going for a walk on the beach. Do you want to come?"

Sophie perked up at that. "I can go with you?"

"Of course, you can," said Cassie. "We wouldn't leave you here by yourself." She said it as though it was a ridiculous idea, though Colt suspected that it would be quite normal for Sophie.

"Thanks. Which beach are we going to? I like the one near the park." She started making her way to the front door, no doubt assuming that they were going to drive into town.

Colt smiled at Cassie. "We like that one, too. We can go there one day if you like, but since we don't have much time together tonight, I thought maybe we could go to this beach." He went and stood in front of the patio doors that opened onto the deck and overlooked the lake.

Sophie ran back and stood beside him. "There's a beach down there?"

"There is," said Cassie. "We have our own path to get to it, too. Do you want to come and see?"

Sophie nodded eagerly.

As they walked down the path, Sophie ran on ahead. Colt took hold of Cassie's hand. "What do you think?"

She looked up into his eyes and smiled. "I think I want this more than almost anything else on earth."

"Only almost?"

She planted a quick peck on his lips. "I want you. I want us."

He put his arm around her shoulders and hugged her into his side. "Same here. But I feel like we already have us. We always did. We just took a bit of a detour. I think we can give her a good life and think she'll make our lives better, too."

"Hurry up, guys! You need to come see! It's awesome!" Sophie shouted.

They exchanged a smile and hurried after her.

Chapter Eighteen

Cassie pulled into a spot near the entrance to the grocery store. She was hoping to be in and out as fast as she could. She didn't like to stop on her way home from work on a Saturday. It was always so busy. But she only needed a few things—she wanted to make a special treat as a Valentine's surprise for Colt.

She called him as she walked across the parking lot.

"Hey, love. What's up?" he answered.

"I'm at the grocery store. Do you want me to get you anything?"

"Nothing I can think of, thanks."

"Okay."

"How are you feeling about things today?"

She smiled. "Like I can't wait until Monday."

He chuckled.

"What?"

"I was hoping you might be looking forward to tonight."

"Oh! Sorry. I am. You know I am." They were going out to the Valentine's dinner at the Boathouse, and of course, she was looking forward to it.

"It's okay. I'm excited about Sophie coming on Monday, as well. I think it's going to be great. But tonight's a special night, too."

"I know. I'm looking forward to it. In fact, I'm preparing a little treat for you."

"Hmm. I like the sound of that. Does it involve you naked?"

Cassie smiled and glanced around. "It could if you'd like."

"You know I would."

"Then, wish granted. In addition to the other little treat. That one's just a sweet one, though."

He laughed. "You're sweet."

"I mean to taste."

His voice was lower, huskier when he spoke again. "I want to taste you."

She felt her cheeks flush as she entered the store. "I'd like that, too."

"You don't sound so sure?"

She laughed. "I will be, once I'm out of the store."

"Oh! Right. Sorry."

"Just hold that thought till we're home?"

"I will. I should be back by five."

"That's good. We'll have some time before we go out, then."

"Yeah ... and I want to make good use of it."

She smiled. "Me, too. I'll see you as soon as you can get home."

~ ~ ~

Colt hung up and put his phone back in his pocket.

"That can only have been Cassie, judging by the smile on your face," said Don.

"It was."

"Have you popped the question yet?"

"No, but I'm working on it."

Don smiled. "What work is there to do? You just ask her. I think we all know what her answer will be."

Colt nodded.

"What? There's not a problem, is there?"

"Hell, no! It's just that I'm trying to figure out when's the best time to do it."

Don made a face. "It's Valentine's day. Strikes me that's as good a time as any."

"Not really. I mean, it's a bit generic, isn't it?"

Don smiled. "And you like to think of yourself as an original."

Colt grinned. "Something like that."

"I know it's not exactly romantic, but if young Sophie's coming to stay with you, don't you think you should do it sooner rather than later?"

"That's what I'm struggling with. I need Cassie to know that I'm asking her to marry me because it's what I want, what I've always wanted—for her to be my wife. I don't want that to get lost in doing it because we need to so that we can get Sophie."

"You don't think Cassie already knows?"

"Yeah, she does, but still …"

Don grasped his shoulder. "It's not the when you do it, but the how."

"So, how do I do it? I'm not big on grand gestures. I know she wouldn't want to share the moment with a bunch of people. But that's about all I do know."

Don shrugged. "I can't tell you. You know her best. Use your imagination. But hurry up about it."

Colt chuckled. "Thanks for your help."

"Do you even have a ring?"

He blew out a sigh. "No. I keep trying to get over to the plaza at Four Mile, but I haven't had time yet."

Don smiled. "Then, that's how I can help. Go."

"What … right now?"

"Yep. Take the afternoon. There's nothing happening here that can't wait. Go and buy your girl a ring." He smiled. "I'm proud of you, Colt."

Colt had to swallow. "Thanks."

Don nodded. "Go on, before either of us embarrasses ourselves."

"I'll see you Monday."

Don smiled. "Yeah, and I'll be making sure you don't get so much overtime from Monday on."

Colt raised an eyebrow.

"Because Sophie's going to want her new daddy at home."

Colt thought about Don's parting shot on his drive over to Four Mile. Sophie's new daddy? Wow. Of course, that was what he wanted to be. Be he had to wonder if he ever would. He and Cassie had had a great time with her last night. She was looking forward to coming to stay with them for a couple of weeks. But when she'd come to collect her, Kelly had made very clear that it would only be a trial period. She'd spoken openly to them and to Sophie about the possibility of it not working out.

It had seemed that Sophie didn't really expect it to. Colt hoped that over the years to come, they'd be able to restore her faith in what family meant. He'd love to think that she'd come to think of them as her mommy and daddy, but more than that, he hoped that she'd come to believe in herself and her own worth. It broke his heart to hear her talk about herself as trash.

He hurried across the square in front of the clock tower. The plaza was busy, considering that it was February. When he reached the store, he pushed the door open and went inside, hoping that it wouldn't be too busy in there. He should have known really—a jewelry store on Valentine's day weekend? There were three couples browsing the display cabinets. He turned around to let himself back out.

"Hey, Colt." Maria called after him.

He turned back and smiled. "Can I help you find anything?"

"No. I'm good."

Laura, who owned the store, gave him a puzzled look. "Is everything okay?"

Jesus. He didn't want her to go worrying that he was here on official business. "Everything's fine. I'll come back. You're busy."

Laura smiled. "You can wait in the back if you like. There's someone there who I'm sure would be glad of your company."

"Smoke's back there?"

She nodded.

Maria came and ushered him behind the counter with a smile. "Go and hang out with Smoke for a while. You don't want to leave empty-handed, do you?" she asked with a grin.

He smiled and shook his head. He really didn't.

Smoke popped his head out of the office in the back and grinned when he saw Colt. "Hey. You coming to keep me company?"

"It looks that way. I was going to leave, but ..."

Smoke laughed. "They've been expecting you for weeks now. They're not going to let you just walk out."

Colt had to laugh with him. "Don't you think these are some strong-arm sales tactics? Holding customers hostage until they buy?"

"It's not about the sale. It's about why you're buying the ring. You are here for a ring, right?"

"I am."

"Then let me be the first to congratulate you."

"Thanks. I haven't even asked her yet."

"But we all know it's a given. Are you going to ask her tonight?"

Colt shrugged. "I don't think so. It seems too ..."

"Corny?" asked Smoke.

"Yeah. That. It's hardly original, is it?"

"No."

"Do you mind if ask what you did? How did you propose to Laura?"

Smoke chuckled. "I don't think that'll help."

"Try me."

"Okay. I refused to speak to her for weeks, then followed her to London and asked her to make a ring for me for her."

Colt had to laugh. "Wow. That sounds like quite a story."

"I like to think it was. It still is." Smoke smiled. "You'll figure out what your story's going to be. From what I understand, it's already a long one."

"We have a lot of history. It's taken us a long time to get it right."

Laura stuck her head around the door. "Maria's just finishing up with her customers. Do you want to come out and start looking?"

Colt looked at Smoke.

"I can't help you. I'm clueless."

"Moral support?"

Smoke got to his feet with a smile. "Sure."

~ ~ ~

Cassie looked around the kitchen when she heard his truck pull into the garage. She was all finished and had even managed to get everywhere cleaned up. He wouldn't suspect that she'd been baking, apart from the smell, she realized. That was a dead giveaway.

He looked tired, but happy when he came in.

"Rough day?" she asked.

"No." He smiled. "It was a good day."

"Anything you want to tell me about?"

"Maybe later." He sniffed the air. "Anything you want to tell me about?"

She laughed. "I want to say maybe later, too. But I know you. You're going to want one while they're still warm."

"Brownies?" he asked, hopefully.

"Yes. Your favorite ones."

"Aww. You're the best. Thanks, Cass."

She shrugged. "I wracked my brain trying to think of a gift to give you for Valentine's day. But you're not an easy man to buy for. And … I don't know. I didn't want to buy you something just for the sake of it. So, I decided to make you something I know you love."

"Thank you, that's so sweet of you."

She eyed the bag he was carrying, and he laughed. "I knew I should have left this in the truck."

"You didn't need to get me anything."

"Yeah, I did. Believe me, this isn't something that I bought just for the sake of it."

She smiled. "Do I get to see it?"

He frowned.

"I'll bribe you with a brownie."

"I'll have to wait then."

She laughed. "It's okay. If you don't want to give it to me now, I don't want to be a brat. You can have a brownie anyway."

He closed his arms around her and hugged her to him. "You're too good to me."

She looked up into his eyes. "I love you, that's all."

"I love you, too."

"What time do we need to be ready?"

He shrugged, and she had a feeling that she knew what he was thinking.

"Do you still want to go?"

"Of course. It's Valentine's day."

She smiled. "So? We don't have to if you don't want to."

"Are you saying you don't want to?"

"I'll be happy to go. But I'd be just as happy to stay home. Just you and me."

He held her gaze for a long moment, then reached a decision. "Yeah. If you really don't mind. I'd rather stay home. I'll cook. I don't expect you to. But I want you to myself. Things are about to change around here. We won't be able to have a romantic dinner at home and wander around naked if we choose once Sophie's here."

"I know."

"On the other hand, we won't be able to go out so much either."

She smiled. "We will, but it'll be different. In fact, Holly called this afternoon to ask if we want to bring Sophie to their kiddie night on Thursday."

"Wow. Do you think it's a good idea?"

"I do. Don't you?"

"Yeah. Now that I think about it, I do. My first reaction was that it might be too soon. But it's probably better to show her straight away what her life would be like with us."

"Exactly. I think we should involve her in each of our lives and start adjusting things so that we all build what will be our family life together."

"You've thought about this a lot, haven't you?"

She nodded. "I have. And to tell you the truth, part of what I was thinking is that I'd rather stay home with you tonight. This could be our last night as just the two of us. I think it's more special to stay here than to go out with everyone else and conform to someone else's tradition."

He smiled and dropped a kiss on her lips. "I couldn't agree more."

~ ~ ~

After they'd eaten, they sat on the sofa, and Colt slid his arm around her shoulders.

"Happy Valentine's Day."

She smiled up at him. "It is a happy day. I'm glad we decided to stay home."

"What, because my cooking is so delicious?"

She laughed. "You know I love a burger every now and then."

"I'm not a great chef, but I plan to cook more. I don't want you to feel that once Sophie's here, it's all going to be on you."

"I don't feel that way. I enjoy cooking; it relaxes me after work. And besides, I'm usually home first, so it makes sense."

"We'll have to see how it all works out, won't we?"

"We will. And it'll all be fine."

"Are you nervous about anything?"

She shrugged. "Lots of things. Mostly about wanting her to be happy here. I'm getting ahead of myself, too. I keep hoping that there won't be any issues with the adoption process. We really need to set up something more permanent for after school. I love that the Murrays have said they don't mind picking her up with their kids for the next couple of weeks, but we need to have something in place for after that."

Colt nodded. "Assuming that she's going to stay with us."

"That's what I mean about getting ahead of myself. What if she doesn't want to stay? What if … I don't know … something else means it can't happen."

"I keep trying to think of what other obstacles we might encounter, but I can't see anything. Kelly said that because both Kayleen and Randy are willing to relinquish their rights, it makes things much easier, remember? We can adopt her."

"I know. But I can't help wondering if something will go wrong."

He hugged her into his side. "It won't. We know we want Sophie to live with us. If that's what she wants, too, then we have to trust that it'll all work out. I think it's about time that things went right for us, don't you?"

"I do. It's funny I was thinking about that, too. And what we said about if things hadn't gone so wrong between us, we might have had a seven-year-old girl of our own by now. We got off track, but we're getting back on it."

Colt nodded and ran his finger over the ring box in his pocket. He hadn't been sure if tonight was the right time to ask, but what she'd just said about getting back on track decided it for him. As far as he was concerned, this was the track he'd always wanted them to be on.

"Are you okay?" she asked.

"I am. In fact, I'm great. Do you want to go down to the beach?"

"Sure. We'll need to wrap up, though. It's freezing out there."

Once they were bundled up with coats and hats and gloves, they made their way down the path to the beach. Colt's heart was pounding in his chest. This was finally it. He felt as though his whole life up to now had been leading toward this moment.

She took his hand and started walking. "I think this might be my favorite place in the whole world."

"I know it's mine," he answered with a smile. And he knew that from tonight on this beach would be even more special to him. "I'm in my favorite place with my favorite person in the whole wide world."

"Aww." She stopped walking and came to plant a kiss on his lips. "Me, too. And soon, we'll get to share this with our other favorite little person."

He nodded. He felt like that was his cue. He took hold of her hand. "Before that happens, there's something that I want to share between just you and me."

She raised an eyebrow and then laughed. "I think it's a bit cold to be doing that out here."

He chuckled. "Is that all you ever think about? We can save that for later. This is even more important."

"What is?"

He sucked in a deep breath and got down on one knee, pulling the box out of his pocket.

Her hand came up to cover her mouth as she smiled down at him, and he could see tears shining in her eyes.

"I feel like I've waited my whole life for this moment, Cass. I didn't want to do it on Valentine's Day, and I didn't want to do it in front of a bunch of people. But I do want to do it right now. Here in our favorite place. Will you finally do me the honor of becoming my wife? I love you. I've always loved you, and I always will. You're the other half of me. My better half. I want to walk beside you for the rest of my days, loving you and building a life together—and a family together." He held up the box and started to get to his feet.

Instead of waiting for him to stand, she got down on her knees in front of him and cupped his face between her hands. "Yes! Of course, I will. You know I love you, but I don't think you have any idea how much. It's been a long time coming, but I can't wait for you to be my husband. I promise I'll do everything I can to make you happy, to be a good wife to you and a good mother to Sophie and all our other kids."

He chuckled and wiped away the tear that rolled down her cheek. "*All* our other kids? How many are we talking?"

She laughed. "Four, maybe five?"

He raised his eyebrows—"You're saying five or six, total? Or, including Sophie?"

"Four or five more. If you're up for it?"

"How about we start with one?"

"Are you up for that?"

He waggled his eyebrows. "I'm sure I will be if we go back inside, and you warm me up in bed."

"I can do that."

They got to their feet, and he held the ring box out. "Are you forgetting something?"

"Oh, my gosh! Yes. Oh, Colt. It's beautiful!"

He took the ring out, and she took her glove off so he could slide it onto her finger.

She held her hand up to admire it, and Colt felt as though it was some kind of sign when the diamond caught the moonlight and flashed brilliantly for a second.

Her eyes widened. "Did you see that?"

He nodded.

She laughed. "Don't ever try to tell me that that moon doesn't shine."

He laughed. "Okay. I won't."

As they walked hand in hand back up to the house, she turned to him with a strange expression on her face.

"Don't tell me you're having second thoughts already?"

She smiled. "Of course not! I was just thinking … I don't know how this is going to sound to you, but I think you'll understand, so I'm going to say it."

"Go on."

"It's just that, I thought when we got engaged, I would feel like we were finally there, you know?"

He nodded. He knew exactly what she meant, and he was glad that she'd brought it up. He wouldn't have for fear that it might sound as though their getting engaged didn't mean everything to him. It did, but now there was something more. "We're still not quite there, are we?"

"No. This is the foundation of everything, but when Sophie's here—when she's here for good, and we're a family—then it'll feel like we've finally made it to where we're supposed to be." She frowned. "Do you know what I mean? I'm not saying that this isn't amazing."

"It's okay. I understand. I feel the same way. We're not just meant to be together … we're meant to have a family. And we're almost there."

She slid her arms up around his neck, and he lowered his head to kiss her deeply.

Chapter Nineteen

"Colt's here."

Cassie was relieved when Abbie buzzed through to let her know. "Send him in, would you?"

A few moments later, he tapped on her door and came in.

"Hey." She got up and went to kiss him.

"Hey. Are you ready?"

She took a deep breath and nodded. "I've barely been able to think about anything else since three o'clock. I hated knowing that she was getting out of school, and someone else was picking her up. I should have been there for her."

"Relax. She's fine with the Murrays. She's used to it."

"I know, but I want her to get used to us. And I keep thinking that maybe I should go part-time. If I finished at three, I could pick her up myself and take her straight home. I think that'd be better, don't you?"

"Maybe. But we'll figure it out. Maybe we can work it so that you get her a couple of days a week, and I get her a couple." He smiled and looked deep into her eyes. "But that's all detail. It'll all shake out. For now, we want to go pick her up and take her home, yeah?"

Cassie's mind was flitting wildly on the short drive to the Murrays' place. "Did you drop the bag off?"

Colt smiled. "I did. I left it with Janine this morning."

"She didn't mind?"

"No, but I could tell she thought it was overkill. She said Sophie's things wouldn't even fill up half of it."

"We knew that. It was just important—or am being silly about it?"

He smiled. "No. It was important to both of us. I'm glad we went and bought it yesterday. It's kind of symbolic, in my mind. When she comes to us, there won't be a trash bag. She's coming with a bag of her own that we got her. It's the first little step to showing her that we don't think she's disposable."

Cassie reached over and squeezed his hand. "Yes. That."

As they walked up the path to the Murrays' front door, it swung open, and Sophie came running out to greet them.

"Hi! I'm all ready to go. I love my backpack. Thank you." She ran back to the house and came out again with it.

Janine Murray smiled at them. "She hasn't sat down since she got back from school. She's way too excited."

Cassie smiled at Sophie. "We are, too."

"Well, I don't mean to be rude, but I have two boys in the back I need to referee." Janine smiled. "I'll see you after school tomorrow, Sophie."

"Okay. Thank you for letting me stay with you."

Janine smiled at her. "You're welcome. I wish you could have stayed with us for longer."

To Cassie's surprise, Sophie came to her and took hold of her hand.

"See you tomorrow." Janine closed the door, and Cassie exchanged a look with Colt. She'd expected what felt to be such a momentous occasion to be bigger somehow. As if someone should have said something to mark just how important this moment was.

Colt winked at her. "Let's go home."

~ ~ ~

Sophie looked as though she might burst with excitement when she saw her bedroom. "This is really where I get to sleep?" she asked.

"It is," Colt told her. "This is your room now."

A shudder ran down his back when he recognized her reaction. She put her hands on her hips and shook her head in disbelief—just like he'd seen Kayleen do. When she looked up at him, though, there was no trace of Kayleen, just an innocent little face filled with hope. "Do you really mean it—that I can stay here with you guys ... for good?"

Cassie went and sat on the bed and patted the space beside her. Sophie went and sat, and Colt joined them, not knowing what she was about to say, but looking forward to hearing it.

"We hope that you're going to stay here with us for good, Sophie."

"What if I'm bad or I get in the way?"

Cassie shot a glance at Colt. "You won't ever get in the way. We want you here. Sometimes, we'll have to work—you know that Colt's a deputy, and I'm a doctor. So, sometimes we have to go out for emergencies. But we'll always make sure that you're taken care of. And you will never be bad. I don't like that word."

Colt flicked her ponytail, and she looked up at him. "You're a good person, Sophie. Don't ever believe that you're bad. I'm sure you'll misbehave sometimes. You're a kid; that's what you're supposed to do."

She smiled at that.

"And we'll let you know when you're behaving in a way that we don't like. But we'll still love you, and we'll still be here for you. And you won't ever be in the way. Understand?"

She nodded slowly. She didn't look convinced.

"What are you thinking?" asked Cassie.

"You two are different."

"Is that good?" asked Colt.

His heart clenched in his chest when she took hold of Cassie's hand and reached for his, too. The cast on her arm only reminded him of the life that she'd lived up to this point. It made him want to do everything he could to make her life better.

"I promise I'll try to be good. I love it here." She glanced at her backpack at the end of the bed. "I love my bag." She looked up at him and then at Cassie and squeezed their hands. "I love you guys."

Colt pressed his lips together and exchanged a look with Cassie, whose eyes shone with tears.

"We love you, too, Sophie."

"Oh, that's pretty!" Sophie touched Cassie's ring. "Does that mean you're getting married?"

Cassie smiled. "Yes, it does."

"That's cool. Will you wear a pretty white dress and everything?"

"I think so. We haven't decided when or where we're going to have our wedding yet."

"Can I come?"

Colt squeezed her hand. "Of course, you can. We want you to be a part of our family."

"We do," agreed Cassie. "In fact, would you like to be my bridesmaid?"

Sophie's eyes widened. "For real?"

"Yes, for real. I would love for you to be my bridesmaid."

"I'd love to be it." Two little lines furrowed her brow.

"What's wrong?" asked Colt.

"I don't have a nice dress to wear. But maybe Ms. Murray will let me borrow one."

"We'll get you one," said Cassie.

Sophie looked up at her, and Colt loved the way Cassie smiled so lovingly. "I have to go shopping for a wedding dress. We can go together and find your dress at the same time if you like?"

Sophie nodded happily. "Okay." Then her smile faded, and she looked up at Colt. "You don't mind?"

He shook his head. He didn't need to ask her to explain. He could guess that anytime her mom had spent money on her, her father or Jimmy, or the other guys she'd dated had complained about it. "I don't mind one little bit. It's important to me that you should both find dresses that you love and feel pretty in."

Sophie blinked and nodded. He caught Cassie's eye over her head. This was a lot of heavy stuff to be getting into on her first night with them. Yes, he wanted to reassure her and make her feel at home, but he also wanted her to just have fun being here.

"Who's hungry?" he asked.

"Me!" said Cassie.

"Me, too."

"Come on, then. Let's go and see what we can rustle up for dinner."

~ ~ ~

"How's it going with her?" asked Holly.

Cassie smiled. "Wonderfully."

"That's so great," said Emma.

The three of them were sitting on Holly's back deck that looked down onto the beach. Colt, Pete, and Jack were running around down there with Sophie, Noah, and little Isabel.

"She's such a sweetheart," said Emma. "I have to admit that I was worried she might be a little … rough around the edges. But she's just so sweet."

Cassie laughed. "She is most of the time. You could have knocked me down with a feather when I heard her yelling in her bedroom the other night."

"What was she yelling about?"

Cassie shook her head. "I hate to tell you. She was screaming. Fuck off, fuck off, fuck off!"

"Oh, my goodness!"

Holly laughed. "What had made her that mad?"

"She wasn't mad. There was a spider in her room, and she thought that was an appropriate way to tell it to leave because she'd had enough of it."

Emma shook her head. "And, we all know how she learned that."

"We do. But that's all behind her now."

"And what's ahead of her?" asked Holly. "Ahead of you guys. Is it going to be a long road to make it official?"

"Apparently, not. Kelly says it's unusual but not unheard of to make an application for a private adoption of an older kid. She's already helped us fill out the initial forms. And Randy and Kayleen are eager to sign her away." She shook her head. "I still just can't imagine what makes a person that way."

"Don't waste any time wondering about it," said Emma. "Just be grateful that they're happy to sign her over. From what I understand, it would be a long, drawn-out process otherwise."

"You're right."

"And have you set a date yet?" asked Holly. "You know there were a lot of disappointed people at the Boathouse on Valentine's day. Everyone thought we were going to get to be there when he proposed, and then you didn't even come out."

Cassie laughed. "Sorry, not sorry. I've waited a long time for that moment. It was more special that we kept it just for the two of us."

"Are you going to have an engagement party?" asked Emma.

"We're thinking about inviting everyone over for a cookout when the weather warms up a bit. And then hopefully, you won't have too long to wait until the wedding."

"Ooh. I like the sound of that," said Holly. "I hope you're going to come to me when you're ready to look for your dress."

"Of course, I am." Holly owned a boutique over at Four Mile and another in LA. "You're the best dressed woman I know. I'm going to need your help. And Sophie is, too. She's going to be my bridesmaid."

"Aww, that's lovely."

"Just let me know whenever you're ready. You can bring Sophie into the store. I have a gorgeous kids' line in. It'll be fun. Do you have any idea of a date yet?"

"We want to wait until the adoption is finalized. Then we'll do something with Sophie, too. Make us all officially family."

Cassie watched as the guys and kids made their way back up the path from the beach. She was glad they'd come over this evening. It wasn't an official kiddie night, but that just meant there were fewer of them—just her and Colt and Pete and Holly and Emma and Jack. That was probably better for Sophie's first time than having Ethan and Marcus running around, too.

She smiled when Colt swung Sophie up onto his shoulders, and she clung to his head as he ran up the rest of the path. They both looked so happy.

They'd moved inside when the sun set. Colt was looking forward to warmer weather when they'd be able to stay out on the beach until later and play with the kids for longer.

For now, they all sat around Pete and Holly's table after a great dinner. He knew that this would become an important part of their lives. They were lucky to have such good friends. He reached out and took hold of Cassie's hand, and she turned and smiled at him.

Pete got to his feet and clinked his fork against his glass. Sophie frowned and scrambled onto Cassie's lap. Colt could only guess why she reacted that way.

Pete grinned at them. "You know me. I can't let this evening go by without saying a few words."

Holly rolled her eyes and looked at Colt and Cassie. "You know he's about to try and take the credit, right?"

Colt laughed. He didn't mind in the least.

"He doesn't need to take it," said Cassie. "I happily give him credit for seeing what I hadn't been able to figure out and getting us back on the right track."

Pete grinned at his wife. "See!"

She groaned, and Jack and Emma laughed.

"Anyway," Pete continued. "Before I was so rudely interrupted, I wanted to propose a toast, to our old friends, Colt and Cassie." He looked more serious as he raised his glass to them. "Joking aside. I'm thrilled that I was able to play a tiny part in helping you find your way back to each other. I wish you every happiness in the world. You both deserve it. And you, little Sophie." He smiled at her, and Colt was glad to see that she smiled back. "I wish you every happiness in your new life. We all hope that you've found your forever home with Colt and Cassie."

Sophie smiled and snuggled into Cassie's lap and took hold of Colt's hand. "Can I really stay with you guys forever?"

"You sure can."

He reached his other arm around Cassie's shoulders. Hoping that he was finally on course to forever with the woman he'd loved since he was a kid and the little girl who'd already stolen his heart.

He had to swallow hard when Sophie reached up and kissed Cassie's cheek and then turned to him and kissed his.

"How long does forever take?" she asked.

Cassie caught his eye, and they both laughed. "Forever takes a while," she said.

"A long while?"

"A whole lifetime," said Colt. And as he said it, he knew that he would spend the rest of his lifetime loving Cassie and Sophie and doing all that he could to make them happy;

;

A Note from SJ

I hope you enjoyed Colt and Cassie's story. Please let your friends know about the books if you feel they would enjoy them as well. It would be wonderful if you would leave me a review, I'd very much appreciate it.

Check out the "Also By" page to see if any of my other series appeal to you – I have a couple of ebook freebie series starters, too, so you can take them for a test drive.

There are a few options to keep up with me and my imaginary friends:

The best way is to Sign up for my Newsletter at my website www.SJMcCoy.com. Don't worry I won't bombard you! I'll let you know about upcoming releases, share a sneak peek or two and keep you in the loop for a couple of fun giveaways I have coming up :0)

You can join my readers group to chat about the books or like my Facebook Page www.facebook.com/authorsjmccoy
I occasionally attempt to say something in 140 characters or less(!) on Twitter

And I'm in the process of building a shiny new website at www.SJMcCoy.com

I love to hear from readers, so feel free to email me at SJ@SJMcCoy.com if you'd like. I'm better at that! :0)

I hope our paths will cross again soon. Until then, take care, and thanks for your support—you are the reason I write!

Love

SJ

PS Project Semicolon

You may have noticed that the final sentence of the story closed with a semi-colon. It isn't a typo. Project Semi Colon is a non-profit movement dedicated to presenting hope and love to those who are struggling with depression, suicide, addiction and self-injury. Project Semicolon exists to encourage, love and inspire. It's a movement I support with all my heart.

"A semicolon represents a sentence the author could have ended, but chose not to. The sentence is your life and the author is you." - Project Semicolon

This author started writing after her son was killed in a car crash. At the time I wanted my own story to be over, instead I chose to honour a promise to my son to write my 'silly stories' someday. I chose to escape into my fictional world. I know for many who struggle with depression, suicide can appear to be the only escape. The semicolon has become a symbol of support, and hopefully a reminder – Your story isn't over yet

Also by SJ McCoy

Summer Lake Silver
Clay and Marianne in Like Some Old Country Song
Seymour and Chris in A Dream Too Far

Summer Lake Seasons
Angel and Luke in Take These Broken Wings
Zack and Maria in Too Much Love to Hide
Logan and Roxy in Sunshine Over Snow
Ivan and Abbie in Chase the Blues Away

Summer Lake Series
Love Like You've Never Been Hurt (FREE in ebook form)
Work Like You Don't Need the Money
Dance Like Nobody's Watching
Fly Like You've Never Been Grounded
Laugh Like You've Never Cried
Sing Like Nobody's Listening
Smile Like You Mean It
The Wedding Dance
Chasing Tomorrow
Dream Like Nothing's Impossible
Ride Like You've Never Fallen
Live Like There's No Tomorrow
The Wedding Flight

Remington Ranch Series
Mason (FREE in ebook form) and also available as Audio
Shane
Carter

Beau
Four Weddings and a Vendetta

A Chance and a Hope

Chance is a guy with a whole lot of story to tell. He's part of the fabric of both Summer Lake and Remington Ranch. He needed three whole books to tell his own story.

Chance Encounter
Finding Hope
Give Hope a Chance

Love in Nashville

Autumn and Matt in Bring on the Night

The Davenports

Oscar
TJ
Reid

The Hamiltons

Cameron and Piper in Red wine and Roses
Chelsea and Grant in Champagne and Daisies
Mary Ellen and Antonio in Marsala and Magnolias
Marcos and Molly in Prosecco and Peonies

Coming Next

Grady

About the Author

I'm SJ, a coffee addict, lover of chocolate and drinker of good red wines. I'm a lost soul and a hopeless romantic. Reading and writing are necessary parts of who I am. Though perhaps not as necessary as coffee! I can drink coffee without writing, but I can't write without coffee.

I grew up loving romance novels, my first boyfriends were book boyfriends, but life intervened, as it tends to do, and I wandered down the paths of non-fiction for many years. My life changed completely a few years ago and I returned to Romance to find my escape.

I write 'Sweet n Steamy' stories because to me there is enough angst and darkness in real life. My favorite romances are happy escapes with a focus on fun, friendships and happily-ever-afters, just like the ones I write.

These days I live in beautiful Montana, the last best place. If I'm not reading or writing, you'll find me just down the road in the park - Yellowstone. I have deer, eagles and the occasional bear for company, and I like it that way :0)

Made in the USA
Middletown, DE
15 April 2020

89398088R00137